M000306432

(

CALAVA
Press

Portions previously published as part of The Talisman Chronicles (2016)

The right of T.M. Franklin to be identified as the author of this work has been asserted by her under the Copyright Amendment (Moral Rights) Act 2000

Cover images by: ©NeoStock - www.neo-stock.com
©zacariasdamata – www.depositphotos.com
©CURAphotography – stock.adobe.com

Cover design by: T.M. Franklin

ISBN-13: 978-0-9985468-9-6

ISBN-10: 0-9985468-9-5

Visit the Author's Web Site at

www.TMFranklin.com

SUPER POWERS

T.M. FRANKLIN

ONE

The shriek of the whistle echoed against the concrete walls as Beck Leighton dove into the pool. He kicked underwater for a beat before slicing across the surface, his stroke strong and sure. He sucked in only two quick breaths on his way across, and he was sure he cut at least a few points off his time on the flip turn. Pouring it on for the final strokes, Beck touched the wall and finally inhaled deeply as he broke the surface and looked to his coach.

"Not bad, Leighton," he said, eyeing the stopwatch. "Still need to work on your rotation, though."

Beck tried to ignore the voice in his head. *You're not good enough. You're worthless. Waste of space.* He gritted his teeth and nodded. "I'll work on it."

Coach nodded. "You'll get it. Drill a little slower until you get it down."

"Slower?"

"Focus on the technique," Coach Wilson said,

eyeing Beck's teammate in the next lane. "You know what I always say. Technique first . . ."

". . . and the speed will come," Beck said, sliding his goggles off before he hoisted himself out of the pool.

"Nice to know someone's listening," Coach said with a grin. He smacked Beck on the shoulder. "That's enough for today. Hit the showers."

Beck frowned. "But I can—"

"I said, hit the showers." Coach gave him a heavy look. "There's such a thing as over-training, you know?"

Beck sighed. "But—"

"No buts. We've had this conversation before, Leighton. I appreciate the commitment, but you need to get home. Study. Have a good meal."

Beck smiled and shook his head slowly. "Yeah . . . yeah. Okay, Coach."

"See you in the morning." Coach turned away and blew his whistle again.

Beck would be there. 5:00 a.m. like always. Half an hour before the rest of the team showed up. A perfect time to work on his rotation.

He showered and dressed quickly, rubbing a towel over his shaved head before he dropped it into his bag. Coach was right about one thing. He definitely needed to study. Beck slung his duffle over his head and across his body and hefted his backpack on a shoulder. Premed would have been tough enough, but adding a minor in Psychology? Well, it was probably a good thing Beck had no aspirations for a social life, because between school and swim team there wasn't time for much of one.

His mind flashed to Wren Galloway for a moment, and he shook his head to clear it. Wren was a . . . possibility at this point, nothing more. He wasn't sure what it was about her that intrigued him so. Sure, she was smart, but he knew a lot of smart girls. She was different somehow. Ever since whatever happened with the police and that guy that died, she'd been subdued. Introspective. Sad.

And he didn't like it on her.

He shook off thoughts of Wren and things he couldn't have—didn't have *time* for, really—on the walk across campus. Beck made his way to the brick, three-story house he called home, unable to keep from glancing at the alley next door where Wren had been attacked, and he'd fought with Ethan Reynolds. Ethan, who he'd shared a couple of classes with freshman year. Ethan, who he'd never had a problem with before he came at him in that alley.

Now, *that* was weird. But there had been a whole lot of weird going on around town lately.

Beck climbed the porch steps and shouldered his way through the door. Some of the guys were gathered around the table studying in the dining room, which was a frequent occurrence. The unofficially dubbed Archie Hall (short for Archimedes) was traditionally home to science majors who were serious about their GPAs. No freshmen. No parties. No slackers. Acceptance was as strict as any fraternity and any new residents were carefully reviewed by the acting board, comprised of the longest-standing tenants in the house. It was worth it, though. In addition to the benefits of living in such an academically-focused house, the rent was subsidized by a grant through the university.

Beck bypassed the study group and headed up to his room on the third floor. It was small, with an angled roof on one side over his desk and a bookshelf that would have fit against the wall if it was only a few inches shorter. He threw his bags on top of the rumpled bed in the opposite corner, remembering to take out his swim gear and drape it over a rod he'd put up on the wall to let it dry. With a sigh he sat at the desk and opened his book.

Deeply engrossed in his Organic Chemistry text, he had no idea how much time had passed when the phone rang. Distracted, he almost let it go to voicemail before he glanced over and saw who was calling. He reached for the phone and fumbled it a little in his haste to answer the call.

"Hello?"

"Hey, son." His dad sounded tired, and Beck could imagine him in his bedroom across town, a cup of tea cradled in his hand. "How's everything going?"

"Good. Fine." Beck stretched and fiddled with his laptop. "Just studying, you know. The usual."

"Classes okay?"

"Fine."

"How's swim team?"

Beck stifled a yawn. "Good. Getting ready for the meet next weekend. You going to make it?"

"Wouldn't miss it."

The silence hung heavily and Beck knew why his father had called. Why he was reluctant to talk about it.

"Any news?" Beck finally asked.

Jacob Leighton sighed heavily and Beck could picture him shaking his head wearily, the creases around his mouth deepening as he frowned. "Nothing yet. The lawyer's working on it."

"He's been working on it for months." Beck scrubbed a hand over his shaved scalp. "In the meantime, she's still in that house—"

"I know."

"—with *her*. Doing who knows what to her—"

"I know, Beckett! You think I don't know? That I don't care? That every fiber of my being doesn't ache to go take Trulee and to hell with the consequences?" Jacob's voice cut through the connection with a crack, fatigue and frustration evident in every syllable.

"Maybe you should," Beck grumbled.

"You know I can't," his dad said, his voice breaking a little. "You know we have to do this right. We have the evidence that your mom is unfit—"

"That's putting it mildly."

"But I'm not Trulee's blood relative, so it's a difficult case to win."

Beck's eyes watered, and he swiped at them quickly. "*She's* her blood relative. Mine, too. She's our *mother*. And she's done nothing but hurt either one of us."

"I know, son. I know. But Child Protective Services has found no evidence of abuse—"

"So she has to be covered in bruises before they do anything? A broken arm or a busted nose?" he snapped. "Not all abuse leaves visible scars. And Tru will never tell them what's really going on."

"She loves your mom, in spite of everything," his dad said softly.

Beck grunted. "Tru thinks if she's good enough, she'll make it better." He cleared his throat and shook his head. "I used to think that, too."

"There's nothing either of you could do," his father said. "This is your mother's problem, not yours."

"Yeah, well, it doesn't feel like that. She's not the one suffering."

Jacob let out a heavy sigh. "We'll get your sister. It's just going to take some time."

Beck nodded, squeezing his eyes shut. "I worry about her."

"I know. So do I. I'm sorry."

Beck's shoulders fell, weighed down with guilt and frustration. "It's not your fault. I know you're doing everything you can."

"Sometimes it feels like that's never going to be enough," Jacob admitted with a sigh.

"Maybe . . . Maybe I should come home—"

"Beck, we've talked about this—"

"The money could hel—"

"Beckett, no," his father said firmly. "You are where you need to be."

It was an argument they'd had many times before. Beck's tuition was paid for by a swim scholarship, but they still had to pay the part of his rent not covered by the university grant, then there were books and lab fees and food, of course. Beck worked during the summer to help, but it wasn't enough to cover the whole year.

"Beck, we're fine." His dad's voice was gentler, like he was talking to a spooked horse. "We're doing everything we can right now. You need to focus on school and swimming. That's your job."

Beck sighed and rubbed his eyes. "Okay," he said quietly.

"I better go. Don't stay up too late. You need your rest."

"Yeah, I know." Beck yawned and got to his feet. "Early practice tomorrow."

"Be careful," his dad said. "I don't know what's been going on lately, but the paper's been full of muggings and assaults around town. The police are stepping up patrols, but watch your back."

Beck fought the urge to roll his eyes. He could take care of himself, but he knew his father worried. "I will," he said.

"And stay out of dark alleys."

"That was one time!" he grumbled, irritated that his dad was bringing up that thwarted mugging. Again. "What was I supposed to do? Ignore a girl screaming?"

His dad snorted, and Beck could picture his lips curling in a wry smirk, dark eyes twinkling. "I don't know. Call 911, maybe?"

Beck fell back on his bed and threw an arm over his eyes dramatically. "Okay."

"I know it's crazy to think the police might be a better option—"

"I said, *okay*, Dad."

Jacob sighed again. "I'm serious, son. Let the professionals handle this kind of thing."

You're worthless. You're weak. You're nothing.

Beck took a deep breath and tried to ignore the echo of voices—*one voice*—in his head. "I will. I promise."

"Night, son."

"Night."

Beck wasn't sure how long he lay there after he hung up, staring up at the light on the ceiling. He felt strange . . . off. No, that wasn't quite the right word. More like nervous. Expectant.

That was it. *Expectant.* Like something was coming, but he had no idea what it was. Maybe it was just all the talk about his mom and Tru. The fact that it all had to come to a head sometime soon.

Or maybe it was something else. Something he couldn't quite put his finger on.

With a heavy sigh, he stood and turned off the light before crawling back into bed, but it was a long time before he was finally able to fall asleep.

"Beck, wait up!"

He turned and hitched his backpack higher on his shoulder, surprised to see Wren Galloway approaching him with a tentative smile. Beck stepped out of the main flow of traffic on the sidewalk and waited for her to catch up with him.

"Hi," she said, a little breathless. "How's it going?"

"Good. How are you?"

"Oh, good. I'm good. Yeah. Couldn't be better." She pushed back a lock of pale hair, spots of color appearing on her cheekbones. "Heading to class?"

"Umm . . . yeah. Calc."

She made a face. "Gross."

He shrugged. "It's not so bad. What are you doing here? I thought you were only auditing psych this quarter."

"Yeah, I . . ." she jabbed a thumb over her shoulder. "Library, you know. Studying."

What in the world was going on? She seemed nervous or something. Shy. Wren Galloway didn't do shy. "Did you need something?" he asked.

"Me? No. No, I don't need anything." She waved a hand, fiddled with the strap of her backpack, then tugged at her hair again. "I just thought we could walk together maybe?"

Beck shrugged, trying to hide the smile pulling at his lips. He'd almost given up on Wren—she'd made it clear she wasn't interested in being friends, let alone anything more when they first met—but after the attack, she'd relaxed a bit. Maybe saw him less as the dumb jock she'd originally judged him to be and decided to give him a chance. She'd agreed to hang out sometime, but this was the first time she'd actually approached Beck, instead of the other way around. He had to admit, he liked it. A lot.

She looked at him, wide blue eyes dropping to the ground when he met her gaze, and he realized he hadn't answered her question in all his internalized high-fiving.

"Sure," he said, a little loud, a little rushed—mentally kicking himself for losing his cool yet *again*—around Wren. He fought the urge to punch himself in the face.

"So, what's your major?" he asked, wincing at the triteness of the question. He might as well have asked her about the weather.

Wren didn't seem to mind, though. "Psych. You?"

"Pre-Med."

She let out a small laugh. "Have I mentioned how sorry I am that I basically accused you of trying to cheat off me?"

He grinned. "Yeah, you might have mentioned that."

She smiled back, then looked away, her cheeks pink. "What kind of doctor do you want to be?"

"Not sure yet."

"One step at a time, I guess," she said, chewing on her lip as she focused on the distance.

"Something on your mind?" he asked, turning sideways to avoid hitting a bike rider going too fast.

"On my mind? No. Not really." She obviously didn't want to talk about it, so he changed the subject.

"Speaking of Psych. How's your paper coming?"

She wrinkled her nose. "It's coming, I guess. Yours?"

"Same. I've got it outlined, but need to research a little more before I start writing."

"Yeah, me too," she said. "You want to maybe study together later? Throw around some ideas?"

Beck eyed her sideways. "Oh sure, now that you know I have a brain . . ."

She laughed. "I need all the help I can get."

"I feel so used."

"Get over it." She bumped him with her shoulder as they neared the math building. "You want to meet up later? When are you done with classes?"

"Swim practice until four," he replied. "How about after that? Maybe grab a bite or something first?"

Wren smiled, and Beck's stomach gave a little flip.

"Sounds good," she said. "I work at the coffee shop until five. Want to meet me there?"

"Yeah, okay," Beck replied. "See you then."

Wren headed off campus, and Beck jogged up the steps and yanked open the door to the math building, glancing back briefly. He smirked when he saw Chloe

Blake and her friend Miranda descend on Wren, chattering excitedly. Girls did that kind of thing, he supposed. At least his sister and her friends always did.

He frowned, thoughts of Tru dragging him out of the contented euphoria of having a semi-date with Wren. He never felt more powerless than when he thought about his sister and the seemingly unending fight to get her away from their mother. He wished he could simply go get Tru and take her home. He wished the judge would see what was obvious to anyone with two eyes and a functioning brain.

He wished his mother would drink too much one night and just keep on drinking until—

Well, his thoughts could get kind of dark sometimes.

Beck stiffened, his hand still on the open door, as an uneasy feeling suddenly hit him. He turned around again, almost certain he was being watched. Wren and her friends were gone, the crowd of students streaming through campus reduced to a slight trickle as the hour's classes began. Still, he scanned the area, eyes narrowed.

A shadow beneath the trees across Barton Lawn caught his attention, and he could have sworn a man stood there. But the wind changed, overhead leaves let the sunlight through, and the shadow vanished.

Nothing.

Beck shook his head and let out a self-deprecating huff. He was glad nobody saw him freaking out. Obviously, thinking about his mother made him edgy. He needed to get a grip before he overreacted and did something stupid, no matter how much he wanted to, deep down inside.

Beck climbed the steps to the second floor and headed to his math class. His father was right, of course. They had to do this legally. By the book. And eventually, Tru would be with them for good.

He refused to think of the alternative.

"Mr. Leighton? You planning on joining us today?" his professor asked as Beck hovered by the door.

Beck nodded and made his way to his seat, trying to focus on differential equations for the next hour, instead of the women in his life.

The town was ripe for the taking.

The people had no idea. Settled and secure in their limited existence, they knew nothing of what they couldn't see with their eyes, comprehend with their miniscule brains.

But they had their uses. Until It was strong enough, they'd have to do. It settled in their jealous breasts, their angry minds, twisting truths and prodding at insecurities. They nearly always resisted at first, but eventually they gave in—let it overwhelm them, let their rage, their fear and hate consume them.

Violence was its greatest victory.

It fed off it, grew stronger with every blow—every word screamed in fury. Every act of vengeance, envy, or greed.

It relished the chaos and counted the hours until It no longer needed them.

Until It would be ready. Strong enough to take what It wanted.

Strong enough to take *everything*.

TWO

"You okay, Bird?" Dylan nudged Wren with an elbow as he set a mocha on the counter and wiped the steam nozzle with a damp towel. "You seem a little distracted."

The bell over the coffee shop door dinged, and she tried valiantly—and fruitlessly—not to check and see if it was Beck.

"Just expecting someone," she said, straightening the paper cups and glancing surreptitiously at the clock. Again. It was only four-thirty, but business had been slow for the past half hour, giving Wren plenty of time to obsess. And worry. And obsess some more.

"Oh really," Dylan said, drawing out the word with an evil grin. "Only in town for a couple of weeks and she's already nabbed a hot date."

Wren fought the blush, but was again unsuccessful. "It's not a date. It's just a study . . . thing." Thing. That was one way to put it, she supposed. Part of a plan to get Beck to join her in this crazy, super-powered world she now found herself in was another.

"Study thing." Dylan pursed his lips with a nod. "Right."

"It *is*."

He held up his hands. "Okay. So who's this *study thing* with?"

Her cheeks flamed. "Just a guy."

"This guy have a name?"

"Yes."

She could feel Dylan's eyes piercing into the side of her head, but refused to look at him, or say anything more. After a few weighted moments, she sighed heavily. "Beck. His name is Beck."

Dylan leaned back against the counter, his eyes narrowed thoughtfully. "Beck . . . Beck . . . tall, black guy? Swim team?" He eyed her sideways.

"You know him?" she asked, surprised.

Dylan shrugged and popped a chocolate covered espresso bean into his mouth. "He comes in some-times," he replied.

The bell dinged again and they both looked over. Wren fought a surge of frustration when Chloe and Miranda walked in. Dylan straightened next to her, and ran a hand through his hair. His eyes were wide, bright, and red spots bloomed on his cheeks. She looked from him to the girls approaching the counter.

"Really?" she said quietly, a smile tugging at her cheeks. "Which one?"

Dylan cleared his throat and avoided her eyes. "I don't know what you're talking about." He busied himself dumping the used coffee grounds and refilling the portafilters.

Wren would get more answers later. For now, she turned her attention on Chloe and Miranda.

"What are you guys doing here?" she asked, putting on a fake smile. "I thought we were going to meet up *later*." She gave them a significant look meant to reiterate their agreement that she'd meet up with Beck alone in an attempt to not overwhelm him.

"I know, I know," Chloe said, waving a hand. "We're not staying. We just—" She cut off as Dylan sidled up next to Wren.

"Afternoon, ladies," he said with a smile. "The usual?" His gaze lingered just a touch on Miranda, and Wren made a mental note.

"Yeah, sure," Chloe replied. "And would you mind if we borrowed Wren for just a sec?"

"I think I can get by," he said, gesturing around the near-empty shop. "I'll bring your drinks by when they're ready."

He waved off Wren's thanks and she came out from behind the counter. "What's wrong? Did something happen?"

Chloe waited until they were seated at a table in the corner before she answered. "I had another vision, and I think it had something to do with Beck."

Wren's stomach gave a nervous swoop. "What happened? What did you see?"

"Nothing particularly helpful," Miranda muttered.

"She's right," Chloe agreed. "It was just flashes. Quick images. A woman in the darkness. Someone screaming."

Wren couldn't stop the shudder that ran down her spine. "Beck?"

"No, not Beck," she replied, teeth gritted in frustration. "I couldn't tell who it was. It was too dark."

"But you think it has something to do with Beck."

"I can't explain it. It's just a feeling."

Miranda leaned over the table to whisper, "Her feelings are usually right."

Dylan took that moment to appear with their drinks, and Wren was distracted from Chloe's disturbing vision by the painful flirtation—if you could call it that—between Dylan and Miranda. He headed back to the counter and Wren arched a brow at Chloe.

"I know. It's pathetic."

"What?" Miranda asked, cheeks flushed hotly.

"Never mind," Chloe replied. "We don't have time to dissect your love life at the moment." She glanced at the clock. "We should go. I just wanted to warn you before you met with Beck. I'm not sure you should. Not alone, anyway."

"What? Why?" Wren asked.

"Because of the vision," Miranda replied. "He could be dangerous."

Wren scoffed. "*I'm* dangerous, in case you hadn't noticed." She tried not to let them see how the words cut, her still-hot guilt over what she'd done burning in her gut. She'd killed a man. And although she knew in her head that it was necessary to save her friends—to save a lot of innocent people—her heart still ached with remorse.

Chloe got to her feet, tugging Miranda with her. "Just stay in public places, okay? And keep your phone with you?"

"I'll be fine," she said. "Beck's a nice guy. He wouldn't hurt a fly."

"A fly's not what I'm worried about," Chloe replied. "Just . . . be careful, okay?"

They left without another word and Wren stared after them, lost in thought. Beck wasn't dangerous, she was sure of it.

But then again, not too long ago, she would have said the same thing about herself.

Beck was about five minutes early to meet Wren at the coffee shop. After swim practice, he'd killed as much time as he could in the library, not wanting to wait around for her where she worked like a weirdo. When he rounded the corner, he spotted Chloe and Miranda coming out of the shop, but they turned and walked in the opposite direction, so he didn't bother calling out to them. He cut diagonally across the street and slipped between two parked cars, taking a deep breath before he opened the door of *A Whole Latte Love*. The bell rang overhead, and he spotted Wren behind the counter. She smiled as he approached.

"You ready?" he asked. "I'm a little early."

"Yeah, no problem," Wren replied. "Just let me go grab my stuff." She disappeared through a doorway behind her and Beck noticed the other barista eyeing him.

"Hey," he said. *Dylan*, according to his nametag. "Beck, right?"

"Yeah. How's it going?"

"Good." He gestured toward the espresso machine. "Can I get you something?"

"Nah, I'm good. Thanks."

Dylan adjusted the steam nozzle and let out a few quick bursts. "So," he said. "You and Wren?"

Beck let out a little laugh. "Me and Wren what?"

Dylan grabbed a towel and slowly wiped down the counter. "She says it's a study thing."

"It is."

"That's good. Studying is good."

"It is." Beck was trying hard not to laugh. The guy was tall, almost as tall as Beck, but probably thirty pounds lighter and hardly intimidating. Still, it was obvious he was looking out for Wren, and he had to respect that.

"Wren's my friend, you know," Dylan said. "And she's new in town, so—"

"Oh my god, Dylan." Wren emerged from the doorway and gave him a little shove. "Stop it right now."

"What?" he asked, blinking innocently. "I was just chatting with your—with Beck, that's all."

She glanced at Beck, cheeks flaming. "Sorry about him."

"It's fine."

"See? He says it's fine," Dylan said, waving a hand toward Beck.

Wren glared at him in response as she came out from behind the counter. "We'll talk later," she said, emphasizing her pointed finger with a glare. Dylan ignored her, whistling as he organized the cup lids, apparently unconcerned.

"Ready?" Beck asked, swallowing a laugh.

"God, yes," Wren muttered, and they walked out of the shop. "How was practice?" she asked after a moment.

"Fine. The usual," he replied. "How was work?"

She smirked. "Fine. The usual."

"Seems like you're settling in just fine," Beck said. "New town. New job. New defender of your virtue."

Wren let out a groan. "Oh my God. You couldn't let it go."

"So Dylan is—" He wasn't sure how to finish the thought, but almost held his breath while she made him wait for an answer.

"Dylan is a *friend*," she said, shooting him a sideways glance. "A rather enthusiastic one, who I think has his eyes on Miranda, if you must know."

"Oh." He tried not to grin. He failed.

Wren didn't comment, though. And she seemed to be fighting a smile as well.

"So that's why they were at the shop," he said.

"Sorry?"

"Chloe and Miranda," he explained. "I saw them leaving the coffee shop as I got there."

"Oh!" Wren chewed on her lip, her cheeks flushing suddenly. "Yeah, right."

That was weird.

"Everything okay?" he asked.

"What?"

"Did I say something wrong?"

"Oh! Oh no." She waved a hand, but wouldn't meet his gaze. "Just thinking about other stuff? I do that sometimes. Think. You know."

"Okay," he said slowly, dragging out the word. Something was definitely up, and Wren definitely didn't want to talk about it. That was okay. Beck could wait. "My place is a few blocks that way." He pointed. "But . . . I guess you know that." *Since you were attacked in the alley next door.*

"Um, yeah," Wren said quietly.

"We can grab my car," he explained. "Unless you'd rather drive yourself—"

"That would be good," she said quickly.

"Okay." He stopped, waiting for her to tell him where to go, then Wren shook her head as if to clear it.

"I mean, it'd be good to take *your* car. I don't have one. I walk everywhere so—"

"No prob—"

"I mean I could call my mom or—"

"No, that's fine. Really—"

"—she's supposed to be at work in—"

"Wren." He grabbed her arm mid-flail. "It's fine. We can take mine and I'll drop you off later. It's no problem, really."

She took a deep breath. "Okay. Great. Thanks."

Why did she seem so nervous? Beck couldn't put

his finger on it, but something was definitely off. This was more than first date nerves—if this even could be considered a first date to begin with. She kept darting glances at him and chewing on her lip, even wringing her hands together from time to time before she seemed to notice and stuffed them in her coat pockets.

They walked in silence to Beck's car as he tried to think of something interesting to say. Or ask. Something to break the awkwardness and maybe show Wren that he was an intelligent, interesting person with more going for him than a spot on the swim team. Something to alleviate whatever was bothering her.

They approached Archie Hall and he was sure he didn't imagine the stiffening of her posture as the alley came into view, his black, hand-me-down sedan parked at the curb next to it.

"You okay?" he asked.

Wren seemed to force herself to visibly relax. "Sure. Of course. Why wouldn't I be?"

He didn't answer, but opened the car door for her and she got in with a small smile. When he finally got behind the wheel, he turned to her. "So, what do you feel like?"

"What?"

"To eat, I mean." *Yeah, so smooth. Great job, Beck.*

"Oh," she laughed. "I don't care. I'm new in town, remember? What's good around here?"

Beck winced. "Well, you basically have three choices. Burgers, pizza, or the Pancake House."

Wren wrinkled her nose. "Not the Pancake House. My mom's working and I won't hear the end of it if we show up together." She flushed, eyes wide. "Not that there's anything to hear about. I mean, we're just studying, but she gets kind of excited about things—"

"It's okay."

"—not that it would be bad if there *was* something. You're a nice guy, but . . ." She looked out the window, obviously embarrassed.

"But what?" This was too much fun. Beck made sure to look offended.

"But nothing!" She threw up her hands. "Just ignore me. I don't know what I'm saying."

Beck fought to keep from smiling. "No, that's fine. You're ashamed of me. I get it."

Wren glared at him sideways. "You're not funny."

He pressed a hand to his heart. "And you wound me yet again."

"Shut up and drive," she muttered. "Pizza."

He laughed, relieved that the tension had been eased a bit. "Yeah, sounds good." He started the car and pulled away from the curb.

"So, did it help?" she asked, after a few minutes. Beck looked over to see her waving a hand over her head. "You know, shaving off the dreads. Has it made you faster in the water?"

"Yeah, I think so. Cut three-tenths off my hundred free anyway."

"I have no idea what that means, but it sounds good."

Beck grinned. "It is. It's good." He shrugged as he turned the corner. "Needs to be better, though, if I'm going to make it to state."

"You'll make it," Wren said quickly, then blushed a little. "I mean, I hear you're good. You know, fast."

"Asking about me, huh?" He grinned.

She rolled her eyes. "You're really very annoying. I'm starting to rethink this whole friends thing."

"Too late. You're committed now."

"I signed under duress."

"Talk to your lawyer."

She laughed, the awkwardness from earlier melting away as they pulled into the parking lot at Francino's Pizza. They shared a medium pepperoni and split the bill—at Wren's insistence—and chatted a little about the research paper they were working on: A critical analysis of Dr. Patrick McMahon's *Saint to Sadist: How Good People Go Bad* utilizing personal anecdotal research as well as at least five published sources.

Yeah. *Right.*

After dinner, they relocated to the school library

and spread out their books and papers on a table in a quiet corner. Beck flipped through his notes to organize his thoughts and turned on his laptop.

"I had the weirdest dream last night," Wren said.

"Yeah?" Beck logged on to the library Wi-Fi.

"Yeah, kind of creeped me out a little. It was about this house—a blue house—and when I went to open the door, all this weird black smoke kind of seeped out through the cracks."

Beck looked up, confused. Wren was watching him closely, almost expectantly. Did she think he could interpret her dream or something?

"Black smoke?"

"Yeah." She sat up, and seemed kind of excited for some weird reason. "Thick black smoke. But it wasn't like, *ordinary* smoke, it was kind of . . ."

She waited, and he wasn't sure what to say other than, "Extraordinary?"

"Yes!" Wren nodded furiously. "Yes, *extraordinary*. Exactly. You know what I mean, then."

"Um. I guess?" This was such a weird conversation. "I really don't know much about dream symbolism and stuff."

Wren seemed to deflate. "Oh. So, you've never had a dream like that?"

Beck shrugged. "No, not really. My stress dreams usually involve being naked in class. Or not being able to swim at a meet or something. Not hard to interpret those."

"No, I guess not." She chewed on her lip, her cheeks pink. "Can I ask you something kind of weird?"

Beck smirked. "Weirder than if I ever had a dream about black smoke?"

Wren flushed. "Yeah. Um . . . okay, this is not—" She sat up straighter. "In for a penny," she muttered. "Can you tell me about the mark on the back of your neck?"

He reached up to touch the star-shaped birthmark now clearly visible since he shaved his head. "What about it?"

"How'd you get it?"

Beck felt his own face heat with a wave of self-consciousness. "I was born with it. Why?"

"Just curious, I guess."

"Okay," he said slowly before turning back to his computer.

"Have you ever—" She paused, chewing on her lip again.

"Ever what?"

She thought for a moment, brow crinkled in concentration. "Ever had a feeling of déjà vu?"

He shrugged. "Sure, who hasn't?"

"No, I mean—" She shook her head in frustration.

"I mean, you think it's déjà vu, but then you realize it's more than that."

Beck closed his laptop, placed his hands on the table, and looked her in the eye. "Wren."

"Yeah?" Her eyes darted to the side anxiously.

"What is this really all about?"

It took a moment for her gaze to return to him, then she just stared at him for a few seconds, although he was pretty sure she wasn't really looking at him. She was thinking about something, gnawing on her lip until it turned red and puffy. He let her think, sat quietly until she took a deep breath and squared her shoulders.

"I need to ask you to do something," she said.

"Okay. What?" He wasn't sure what he expected, but it definitely wasn't what came out of her mouth.

"I need you to come to Chloe and Miranda's house. With me."

With all that setup he half expected her to ask him to duel for her honor or change her oil or something.

"Chloe and Miranda's?" he asked, certain confusion was evident on his face.

"Yeah."

"Why?"

"I need to show you something."

"At their house?"

"Right."

"And I don't suppose you want to tell me what that something is?" he asked.

Wren sighed. "It's really something you have to see for yourself." She fiddled with her pen, clicking it a few times. "I swear it's not something weird. Well, I mean, it's *kind of* weird, I guess, but not like *Come check out the severed heads in my freezer* kind of weird."

Beck snorted. "Well, that's a relief."

Wren covered her face with her hands, murmuring to herself before sweeping her hair back and giving him a level look. "Okay, I know this is all really strange, but I swear it's important. I'm pretty sure—I think you—" She shook her head, obviously frustrated. "I can't explain it all now, but I will. Just . . . will you come with me? Please?"

Yeah, it was strange. Wren was kind of strange. Thing is, Beck kind of dug it. He dug her.

"Okay," he said. "When?"

Wren winced. "Now?"

"Now?"

"Yeah." She watched him, her hands clenched so tightly in front of her that her knuckles were white.

He gathered up his books and stuffed them in his backpack, not sure if he was more embarrassed or irritated. "Okay, let's go to Chloe's," he said. "But next time you can ask me outright, you know? You don't have to go through all the hair flipping and *Can we study together* stuff."

"I wasn't—"

"It's fine."

To his surprise, Wren looked outright indignant. "It is *not* fine," she snapped. "I am not one of those mindless blonde bimbos who bats her eyelashes to get what she wants."

"I never said—"

"Yeah, you did. Maybe not in so many words, but you did." In the silence that followed, Beck could hear her breathing shakily, but he didn't meet her eyes. He didn't know what to think. He felt like an idiot thinking Wren maybe liked him, when she really wanted something from him, whatever it was.

"I meant it," she said quietly. "The studying and the hanging out. Beck, I . . . I do like you, okay?"

He glanced up to find her studying her pen, twisting it between her fingers, and a rush of relief swept through his chest.

"You don't sound too happy about that fact," he said, unable to keep back a wry smile.

Wren rolled her eyes. "Well, you're kind of a jerk, sometimes."

"Only *sometimes*? I'd say we're making progress."

"Oh my God." She shook her head. "More than sometimes. *Most* of the time—"

"No, no, you said *sometimes*. No take backs." Beck grinned, enjoying her discomfort immensely.

"*No take backs?* What are you, twelve?"

"You *like* me. What does that make you?"

Wren stood and threw her backpack over her shoulder. "I'm regretting this friendship already. I'm regretting everything. I'm regretting my life."

She turned to stalk away and Beck quickened his step to catch up, throwing an arm over her shoulders. She didn't shrug it off, but she also didn't look at him and her face burned bright red. He decided to give her a break and tell her the truth.

"Just for the record," he said, leaning down to speak into her ear. "I like you, too."

Wren didn't say a word, but her lips quirked up—just a little—and Beck slid his arm from around her and found her hand, linking their fingers.

She didn't pull away.

THREE

Beck found a parking spot in front of the Alpha House, his eyes immediately drawn to the blue Victorian across the street, for some reason. He got out of the car without looking away from it, taking in the peaked roof, front porch, and elaborate stained-glass window taking up a good portion of the first floor.

"Ready?" Wren asked, her quiet voice jolting him out of his examination. He'd been distracted, almost in a daze, and it took him a moment to respond.

"Yeah," he said with a crack in his voice. He followed Wren up the walkway, feeling a strange sense of déjà vu, for some reason. She lifted her fist to knock, and for no apparent reason, he grabbed her wrist to stop her.

She swallowed, obviously nervous, although he didn't know why. "What's wrong?" she asked.

Beck couldn't explain it. It wasn't something *wrong* per se, just an odd feeling of inevitability or anticipation or something. Like something was about to change, although he didn't know what or how. He let Wren go, and his hand trembled as he stuck it in his pocket.

"I don't know," he whispered. "Something feels—"

Wren nodded, like she expected it somehow. "It's okay. It'll be okay. I promise."

Beck wasn't sure he believed her, but he stood back as she knocked on the door anyway. Chloe answered, looking between them both with a questioning expression.

"Everything okay?" she asked.

Wren shrugged. "I guess we'll see."

"Did you tell—"

"I think it's better to just show him," Wren replied firmly, despite Chloe's nervous glance in his direction.

Chloe shrugged and stepped back to allow them in. To his surprise, instead of heading to the living room, Wren started up the stairs. He hesitated, but Chloe held out a hand to direct him to follow, so he did. He heard her close the front door behind him, her soft treads on the steps as she took up the rear of their strange little group.

Wren didn't hesitate when she got to the second floor, but continued down the hall and up a ladder Beck assumed led to the attic. A muted anxiety raced along his skin, his stomach fluttering with a nervousness he couldn't explain, and he rubbed a hand over his head, just for something to do with it. He didn't ask questions, not wanting to disrupt the hush that had fallen over them. Instead, he put one foot in front of the other, climbed the ladder and emerged in the sloped-roof attic, brushing dust off his hands and looking toward Wren expectantly.

She waved a hand toward the far corner. "Do you see anything unusual over there?" she asked.

He followed the motion, his gaze sweeping over the expected contents of an attic—stacks of boxes, luggage, pieces of furniture—and settled on a wooden chest that seemed as if it belonged there, but was still strangely out of place.

"He feels it," Chloe whispered.

"I know."

"Feels what?" Beck's sharp words cracked in the quiet room. "What are you guys talking about?"

"You need to explain it to him first," Chloe told Wren.

She huffed out a humorless laugh. "How?"

"He needs to know what he's getting into."

"Again, I ask . . . how?" Wren said with a glare.

Chloe glared right back. "Show him."

"I swear to God," Beck growled. "If somebody doesn't tell me what's going on, I am walking out that door."

"Okay!" Wren threw up her hands. "Okay . . .

just." She took a deep breath and turned to face him. "Look at me, all right?"

"But-"

"*Look at me.*" Wren reached out to grab his upper arms. "I promise, this will explain everything—or at least give us somewhere to start."

Beck still didn't have a clue what she was talking about, but he stilled, watching her carefully. "Okay."

She stepped back, releasing his arms. "Don't take your eyes off me."

"I said *okay*. Would you—"

But then, in the blink of an eye—less than that, since Beck didn't even blink—she was gone. Disappeared right in front of him. *Poof.*

He barely registered Chloe's smug look before he spun around and found Wren on the other side of the room, sitting on an old dresser.

"What the—"

Then she was gone again, appearing back where she'd been before and watching him with nervous eyes.

"How—How did you—" He couldn't even form the sentence, unable to believe what he'd just witnessed. Beck suddenly felt a little lightheaded, and he slumped into a rickety old chair, dust puffing up around him. When it settled, he bent over, head between his knees and breathed deeply. The others didn't say a word, just let him get ahold of himself, and eventually, he sat back up and looked at Wren.

"What was that? How did you do that?" he asked. "Did I just see—" Maybe he'd hallucinated. That made as much sense as anything, really.

"You did," Chloe replied quietly.

Wren took another deep breath, like she was preparing herself. "I can manipulate time," she said finally.

"Time."

"Right."

"You're telling me you can manipulate time."

"Yes." She shrugged. "More like freezing it for a bit. I've been working on speeding it up and slowing it down. The slowing down is easier, I guess because it's more like freezing, which is the easiest. But—"

Beck burst out laughing. "Right. Of course it is." He leaned back into the chair and it creaked under his weight as he snorted. "Freezing is the easiest. That makes *perfect* sense."

"She's telling the truth," Chloe said, brow furrowed as if annoyed by his laughter.

"Come on, you guys. Enough's enough." Beck wiped tears from the corners of his eyes. "What's really—"

"You almost wore a white t-shirt this morning," Chloe said, eyeing his blue one. "You had it on, but you spilled something on it. Something red. Ketchup, maybe? So you had to change."

Beck stilled. "How could you—how could you know that?"

"Chloe sees things," Wren replied. "She gets visions."

Beck swallowed. This wasn't so funny anymore. "That's . . . not possible."

"You threw it toward the hamper, but you missed," Chloe said. "Overshot it—guess that's why you don't play basketball."

The lightheadedness was coming back. Beck forced himself to breathe evenly, steadily. There was no way Chloe could have known that. He was alone in the house. Alone in his room. Unless . . .

"Did you hack my webcam or something?"

Wren snorted. "Chloe doesn't know the first thing about computers."

"Hey!"

"It's true."

Chloe frowned. "I know, but you don't have to say it like that."

It didn't matter. Beck knew that wasn't possible anyway. His laptop had been packed away in his backpack. He'd just run up to switch shirts—already running late—and threw the dirty one toward the hamper, no time to grab it when he missed.

"Tabasco," he said. This was too much. It was *impossible*. But—

"What?" Wren asked.

"It was Tabasco. Not ketchup," he replied. "I spilled Tabasco sauce on my shirt this morning. That's why I had to change.

"Now I think you guys need to start from the beginning," he said. "And please, go slow."

So they did. They told him about Chloe's house, and the window—her visions of the past, present and possible future—*That seems like it would be kind of frustrating, he said. You have no idea, Chloe replied.* Beck took it all in with shocked incredulity that slowly twisted into cautious acceptance after a few more examples of their unbelievable abilities. Regardless of how outlandish the story was, he could find no other explanation. It was impossible, but he slowly realized it was true. It had to be true. And as soon as he thought the words, let the doubt ease just a little, he realized he believed it. He believed *them*, or at least he was beginning to.

They told him about the wooden chest and Wren's gift, about the vision Chloe had of him in the middle of some great battle against a giant smoke monster—Wren's words, not his—and finally about her most recent vision: Beck sitting there, with them at that moment in the attic before opening the chest in the corner for himself.

"So, you're saying it's inevitable." He glanced sideways at the chest in the corner. "I'm going to open it."

"You have a choice," Chloe replied. "You could leave right now and never come back. I only see what *could* be."

"And if I open it, what then? What happens?"

Wren sighed. "We don't know for sure."

"But you have an idea."

Chloe nodded slowly. "It's Miranda's idea actually. She thinks the chest appears for those who are chosen."

"Chosen by who? For what?"

"Who? We have no idea," Chloe replied, shaking her head. "As for what? To fight, we think." She took a seat across from him on a rolled up rug. "That smoke . . . thing . . . it can enter people. Make them do crazy things." Chloe rubbed her eyes. "We don't know what it is. What it's going to do next. But Wren's gift helped stop it once. At least for a while."

"But it's not gone forever," Wren added. "And if Chloe's vision is right, it's going to get stronger until, at some point, it will take more than us—a lot more—to defeat it."

"We think maybe you've been chosen, too," Chloe said. "For a gift. One that will help us fight."

"And the gift is in the box?"

"That's the theory," Chloe replied. "If you decide to accept it."

Beck thought about that for a moment. "But if I don't open it. If I choose not to then I wouldn't be there, at that fight in the field, right?"

"I don't know," Chloe said honestly. "Probably not."

"And you two will."

"Yeah." Wren shrugged. "We've kind of accepted that."

The idea of the two of them facing whatever that smoke monster was—what it could do—did not sit well with Beck. There was no way he'd turn and run if they were going to stand and fight. He stood up and stretched. "Well, I can't let you guys have all the fun."

Chloe got up as well, and Wren grabbed his wrist. "Are you sure about this?"

Beck grinned. "Hey, fate has spoken . . . or whatever."

"You have a choice," Chloe said again.

"I know. I know." Beck nodded, waving a hand dismissively. "And it looks like I'm making it."

He walked to the chest and glanced at them over his shoulder. "So I just open it?"

"Yeah." Wren gripped Chloe's hand, knuckles white.

Beck, never one to delay ripping off the Band-Aid, flipped the top open and looked inside.

"What do you see?" Wren asked, and he realized they'd both approached and were looking over his shoulders.

"Just an old glove," he replied. "You don't see it?"

He could feel them shake their heads although he didn't look up. The glove was worn black leather, long enough to fit up over his wrist by several inches. It lay crumpled in the corner of the box, discarded and forgotten.

"So, I should pick it up," he said—not a question, so they didn't answer. The tension in the room ramped up another level, the silence of held breath making Beck's heart pound. He reached in and grabbed the glove.

A white light shot out of the chest, enveloping him and making him squint. He only felt the soft leather in his palm for a moment. It quickly became a warmth—a tingling melting between his fingers like hot wax—and as he watched, the glove vanished before his eyes. His right hand glowed, pulsing lightly, and he held it up to examine it with awe. A glove of light enveloped his fingers, his palm, up over his wrist to the middle of his forearm. It sparked thoughts of knights and armor—a medieval gauntlet gripping a sword or a lance.

Then, just as quickly as it appeared, the light dissipated and he was left staring at his hand, flexing it tightly against the remnants of prickling heat until they evaporated as well.

He started, looking up to find Chloe and Miranda were both watching him with mouths dropped open.

"So," he said. "That was interesting."

"Do you . . . feel anything?" Wren asked.

"Like what?"

She shrugged. "I don't know. Anything."

He finally lowered his hand and took stock of his body, tilted his head, rolled his shoulders, took a few steps and raised his eyebrows.

"I don't really know what I'm supposed to feel."

Chloe approached him slowly, but stopped at arm's distance. "Maybe it has to sink in."

"What does?"

"It happened right away with me," Wren countered.

"Maybe it's happening and we don't know it's happening," Chloe replied.

Beck huffed. "*Nothing* is happening. I'd know if something was happening."

"Would you?" Chloe narrowed her eyes.

"Wouldn't I?" He looked at Wren, who shrugged. No help there.

Beck's phone buzzed and he frowned, thumbing open a text from his dad. How could he have forgotten the meeting with CPS?

"I've gotta go," he said, heading for the ladder.

"I don't know if that's such a great idea." Chloe rushed to catch up to him. "Until we know what's going on with you, maybe—"

"I'm fine," he replied, hurrying down the ladder and striding toward the stairs. "I've got to get over to my dad's. There's . . . stuff I have to deal with."

Maybe it was all over. Maybe Tru was theirs, finally. He threw open the front door.

"But—"

He whirled on Chloe. "Look, I really have to go. I promise, if time stops or moves backward or I start flying or shooting lightning out of my fingers, I'll let you know right away, okay?"

"Lightning," Wren murmured. "That would be cool."

"Can we please focus?" Chloe snapped, throwing her hands in the air. She took a deep breath and pointed at Beck. "You will call us if anything —*anything*—out of the ordinary happens. No matter how small."

Beck's lips twitched. "Yes, ma'am."

"Shut up," she grumbled.

He jumped down the front steps, pausing only to call over his shoulder. "I don't feel anything anyway. Maybe nothing's going to happen."

They both looked doubtful, but Beck smiled and

waved as he headed toward his car. Nothing was going to happen. Magic boxes and super powers and smoke monsters. *Oh my.*

It was all so ridiculous. So impossible. Crazy.

Nothing was going to happen.

Except that it did.

Beck barely managed to stay under the speed limit as he raced to his father's house, concern over his sister pushing aside the odd events of the past hour. He parked in the driveway, and jogged up the front steps, calling out as he slammed through the door. His father emerged from the kitchen, face drawn and haggard, and all Beck's hopes dwindled in a flash.

"What is it?" he asked, slumping against the wall.

His dad sighed. "Another delay. It'll be at least a month before we can go to court."

"*A month?* You've got to be kidding me." Beck dropped his backpack and rubbed at his forehead. "They have the psychologist's report, right?"

"Your mom has her own psychologist."

"What about my testimony? Isn't it worth anything?"

"They say I could have coerced you."

Beck tightened his jaw. He could feel his teeth

grinding. "That's ridiculous. You're not the one who plays mind games."

Jacob pulled a chair away from the dining room table and sat down with an exhausted huff. "I know you're disappointed."

"I'm more than disappointed," he replied. "But this isn't about me. It's about Tru."

"I know."

"It's about keeping her safe. It's about getting her away from—"

"I *know*, Beck. I wish I had better news."

Frustration and anger twisted in Beck's stomach, heating his skin. "I don't understand how they can leave her there. It's not right. Anyone who spends more than five minutes with her would see that." He kicked his backpack, and to his surprise, it shot across the floor, nearly to the kitchen door. He was vaguely aware of his hand tingling and clenched his fist against the sensation.

"Beckett . . ." Jacob slumped in his chair, unable to console him.

Beck shook his head slowly, the fury burning through him. "Can't they see through her lies?" he asked. "She puts on a dress and a smile and charms her way past all the social workers and psychologists. Why can't they see through it? See through her?" His hand almost throbbed now, but he barely noticed.

"Beck, calm down."

"No!" He spun on his heel and headed for the door. "I need to get out. I need to think." He tightened his grip on the doorknob, surprised to see a soft glow appear around his fingers . . . a glove of light. Shocked, he shoved that fist into his pocket and opened the door with his other hand. "I'll be fine," he muttered. "I'll call you later."

His dad sighed again, defeated. "Please do, okay? I want to make sure you got home all right."

Beck nodded and all but shot out the door. He looked up and down the street then ducked into his car, holding his breath as he pulled his hand out of his pocket.

Nothing. The glow was gone. He blew out a slow hiss of relief, then he pulled his phone from his pocket to send a quick text.

Something happened.

FOUR

They met at a park about a block from Chloe's house that was busy during the day but after dark was pretty much empty. Streetlights cast long shadows of playground equipment across the ground, and the ball field hovered in that semi-eerie state of half-lit, half-darkness.

"So, it just started glowing?" Chloe asked.

"Yep."

"And nothing else?" Wren watched him carefully.

"Like what?" Beck noticed she'd clenched her own hand into a fist.

She shrugged. "Like . . . tingling? Itching? Any kind of feeling to go along with the light show?"

"No—" Beck started to shake his head, then froze. "No, wait. Yeah. Yeah, there was some tingling . . . and heat." He lifted his hand and wiggled his fingers. "What do you think it means?"

Wren exchanged a glance with Chloe. "It's what

happens to me," she explained, holding up her own palm. "I get a tingling feeling and the watch starts to glow."

Beck's eyes widened as the image of a clock face appeared on Wren's hand, pulsing lightly. She closed her fingers around it and the glow faded after a moment.

"But then time stopped," Chloe pointed out. "At least the first few times you had no control over it, but for Beck, nothing else happened."

Wren thought for a moment, chewing on her lip. "Are you sure about that?" she asked him. "Nothing out of the ordinary? Do you remember anything about what you were feeling right before it happened? Maybe we can replicate it."

Beck considered that. "I was . . . mad."

"How mad?"

"Pretty mad," he replied, remembering how he'd felt when his dad had told him Tru would be stuck with their mother for the time being. "Furious, actually. And frustrated."

Wren nodded, turning to pace a little on the damp grass.

"What do you think it means?" Chloe asked.

"Emotions," Wren replied, stopping just short of a pool of light. "Fear. Frustration. For me . . . I was overwhelmed and wanted everything to stop. And it did."

"But nothing stopped for Beck," Chloe said.

"No, but . . ." Beck scrubbed a hand over his head, thinking . . . remembering . . . There was something. "I kicked a backpack. I didn't really think about it at the time, but . . ."

"But?" Wren prompted.

"It kind of went a long way. I mean, I didn't kick it that hard, but it slid all the way into the kitchen."

They moved to stand in a loose circle, absorbing the information. Unsure what it all meant.

"So what now?" Beck asked.

Wren shrugged. "Now, I try to teach you to focus, and we figure out exactly what gift that box has given you."

"Okay, so how do we do that?"

"Umm . . . close your eyes." Wren looked uncertain, but Beck figured she was the best he had, so he did as she said.

"Now, try to think back to how you were feeling at that moment. What set you off?"

Beck rolled his shoulders. "I was talking to my dad. About my little sister."

"I didn't know you had a sister."

Beck opened his eyes to find Wren flushing.

"Sorry," she said, looking away.

"It's okay. It's kind of a long story. She lives with

our mother," he replied. "That's kind of what I was mad about."

Wren opened her mouth, and he could tell she wanted to ask more, but instead she nodded.

"Okay, so think back to how you were feeling. I think the first step is trying to recapture those emotions."

Beck closed his eyes again and took a deep breath as he tried to follow her instructions. He thought about Tru, about the battle to get her away from their mother.

About the lawyers. The court. The endless hearings and evaluations.

About the waiting.

About the pain. The frustration. What Tru could be going through at that very moment.

The endless criticism and humiliation. The taunts and emotional abuse.

Anger curled in his stomach and twisted through his chest and he let it grow, let it flow unchecked into a ball of white hot fury. Beck was vaguely aware of a tingling in his right hand.

His fingers twitched.

"Whoa," Chloe murmured, and his eyes flew open.

Both girls were staring at his hand and he lifted it to find it once again enveloped in a glove of light. He wiggled his fingers loosely.

"Now what?" he asked through gritted teeth, the anger still pulsing through him.

"Umm . . . try to do something?" Wren suggested.

"What?"

"I don't know."

Beck glared at her. "I thought you knew what you were doing."

Wren glared right back. "Well, you thought wrong. We're all trying to figure this thing out."

"Great!" Beck snapped, waving his arm, the light trailing behind his movement. "In the meantime, I'm a walking glow stick!"

"I think we should all just calm down," Chloe interjected.

"Calm down?" Beck stalked toward the swing set as the tingling in his hand intensified. "How am I supposed to calm down? My family's a mess, my sister's in trouble, and I look like I've been possessed by a black light poster."

He smacked the swing set in frustration. "Not—"

A creaking interrupted his thoughts and it took a moment for Beck to absorb where the sound had come from. The swing set shuddered, the support post bent neatly into a ninety degree angle where he had hit it. With a loud groan and clatter of chains, the whole thing swayed forward and Beck scrambled back as it collapsed onto the bent post. He stared at the crumpled metal, mouth dropped open in shock as the tingling eased in his hand and the glow faded away.

The silence that followed hung heavy around them, broken only by Beck's uneven breaths and the lingering rattle of the one swing still hanging crookedly from the remaining posts.

"Well," Wren said clearing her throat when it came out as a croak. "I guess we know what you can do."

Beck looked at her wide-eyed. "I'm sorry," he all but squeaked. *What did he do? What was going on?*

Chloe stepped forward. "I think maybe that's enough for tonight," she said, glancing at the crumpled swing set. "We should get out of here."

The distant whine of a siren broke Beck out of his stupor and he stumbled after them toward the parking lot.

"That can't be for us. It's not for us, right?" Wren asked, worry lacing her tone.

"The siren? No, I don't think so," Chloe replied. "There's a lot of stuff going on in town lately. People are nuts. Must be a full moon or something."

They stopped at Beck's car and he hesitated at the door. "What should I do now?" he asked, still more than a little bewildered.

Chloe took him by the shoulders. "It's going to be okay," she said, shaking him slightly. "Go home and get some sleep. Tomorrow after class, we'll work with you and figure out how you can control it. In the mean-time . . ." She glanced at Wren.

"In the meantime?" Beck prompted.

She shrugged. "In the meantime, try not to freak out. And try not to get mad."

"Right." Beck nodded, his head loose on his shoulders. "Right. Yeah, sure."

He got into his car and squeezed the steering wheel as he watched the girls head for Chloe's house.

Don't get mad. Don't freak out. Easier said than done.

A woman stood at the edge of the playground, concealed in the shadows of a few evergreen trees. She shifted restlessly on her feet as she watched the boy start his car and drive out of the parking lot. She was nondescript—middle-aged, slightly overweight, wearing loose, colorless clothing and sensible shoes, with skin once the color of creamy coffee now sallow and faded, neat braids springing loose in frizzy, sporadic tufts.

The kind of woman people rarely noticed.

Which was why It had chosen her, of course.

"What do I do now?" she asked, eyes on the boy's taillights as he turned and headed down the street.

"Nothing," It replied. "It's too late to stop him now. He's already claimed the gift."

She waited, knowing It would instruct her further. Nervously, she thumbed at the wedding ring on her left hand, spinning it around and around.

"I'm hungry," It said.

She turned to tromp listlessly down the street toward the middle of town, the scream of police sirens a potent lure to the thing inside her.

Beck had a headache before his first class had even started the next day. Having barely slept, he slogged through early practice, gaining seconds on his lap times and criticism from his coach. Coffee and aspirin helped him focus during class, and he was grateful that he had a three-hour break after lunch so he could grab a quick nap before afternoon swim practice—or at least toss and turn for a couple hours, managing maybe a half hour of sleep. By the time he emerged from the locker room that afternoon, all he wanted was to go back to bed and forget everything. Or go back in time a couple days before he'd ever opened that chest . . . or heard about this battle he was evidently destined to be a part of.

Maybe Wren could help him out with that.

"I don't time travel," she said with a roll of her eyes when he asked her. "And that's not really a solution to your problem, anyway."

"I know," he mumbled.

They'd met at Chloe and Miranda's house, which was apparently where all this super-secret, superhero training went on. They were the only two occupants of the huge Victorian, but Miranda said their landlord insisted the place would fill up quickly. Beck didn't know about that. They were months into the school year, so he wasn't sure where all these tenants were supposed to be coming from.

Miranda, he'd learned, was in the know on the whole mystical window premonition, mysterious chest of super powers thing, but apparently hadn't been chosen by the chest, or whoever—or whatever—was in charge of such things. She'd opted out of training, saying she was going to be doing research, whatever that meant. She headed up to her room while Chloe led Wren and Beck out to the garage, where she rolled out an ancient set of barbells.

"Best I could come up with on short notice," she said as she straightened, dusting off her hands. "They look like they've been here forever, but they should do the job."

Beck rounded the barbell, eyeing the weights on

either end. "How much is on here?" He gave it a tentative tug, but couldn't lift it.

"Everything I could find," Chloe replied. "I hope it's enough."

"It's enough," Beck said, trying to pick it up again and failing.

Wren stood across from him. "So, we need to work on helping you to access this strength, without having to get so angry."

He rolled his shoulders. "And how do I do that?"

Wren chewed on her lip. "For me, it's about focus. You need to think about how the power feels, separate from the emotion. You know—the tingling in your hand—that kind of thing. For me, it's like an electric shock, almost."

"Yeah . . ." Beck nodded, remembering the feeling. "But not a zap, more like the current is kind of flowing through you."

"That sounds pleasant," Chloe muttered.

Wren shot her a look. "Not helpful."

"Sorry."

Wren turned back to Beck. "So, try to recapture that feeling," she told him. "Imagine it until you feel it."

"Fake it until you make it?" he said with a lopsided grin.

"Something like that."

Beck swallowed. "I meant to say . . . I'm sorry, you know, for biting your head off last night."

"It's okay."

"I didn't mean it. I wasn't mad at you."

"I know." Wren smiled softly. "Really, it's okay. I get it. This whole thing is pretty overwhelming."

They locked eyes and Beck felt his face grow hot under her gaze. He cleared his throat and looked away. "Okay then, imagine the tingling. Check."

"Visualize it," Wren suggested. "Think about the feeling, and the light. Try to picture it in your mind."

Beck nodded, his brow furrowed as he concentrated. He tried to follow Wren's murmured instructions, wiggling his fingers slowly as he focused on the memory of what he'd felt the night before—laying aside the anger and frustration as he centered his thoughts on his hand—the tingling and the light. The electricity flowing out from his fingers, up his arm and through his body. The surge of strength that came along with it, making him feel awake . . . more aware of everything around him. It took more than an hour, but eventually, he felt the beginnings of an electric pulse in his fingertips.

"That's it," Chloe said quietly.

At that, Beck's focus faltered and he opened his eyes just in time to see the light fade from around his hand. He let out a defeated sigh and cursed under his breath.

"Don't feel so bad," Wren said, reaching out to squeeze his arm. "You did great. It'll just take practice. It gets easier, I swear."

Beck nodded, not one to give up or shy away from hard work. He knew what it took to develop a skill— knew from long hours in the pool—that becoming good at something wasn't only about gifts and talents, but about being willing to put in the time and effort to make it happen.

He closed his eyes and tried again.

———

Beck collapsed onto his bed with a jaw-cracking yawn that night, more tired from the constant mental exercise of visualization than from swim practice. He stared sightlessly at the ceiling, more than a little disappointed at his showing. By the time he left Chloe's, he'd been able to maintain the light around his hand for close to a minute, but as soon as he tried to lift the barbells, it would fade. He'd yet to be able to draw on the hidden strength that the glove had apparently given him.

He frowned when his phone chimed, Tru's familiar ringtone playing merrily. He glanced at the screen before answering, wondering why she'd be calling so late, and worried about what that could mean.

"Tru?"

"Hey, big bro," his sister's melodic voice greeted him.

"Is everything okay? Are you okay?"

Tru laughed. "Relax, Beckett. I'm fine. Can't a girl call her brother to say hello when she hasn't seen him in *forever*?"

Beck forced himself to relax back into his pillow. "You know that's not my choice. The lawyer said—"

"I know, I know," she replied, and he could picture her rolling her eyes. "It's better for the case if you stay away. I've heard it before."

"It'll be over soon."

"We hope."

"Yeah." Beck sighed. "I know it's taking forever, but Dad says we need to play by the rules if we have any hope of him winning custody."

He heard a rustle of fabric and imagined Tru was probably in her room as well, curled up in bed.

"I know," she said quietly. "It's just hard, you know?"

"Yeah." He took a deep breath, almost afraid to ask the question. "Seriously, Tru, are you okay?"

She hesitated just enough to make him worry.

"Tru?"

She lowered her voice, almost whispering into the phone. "I'm okay."

"Is she there?"

"She's in her room."

"Drinking." It wasn't a question.

"It's not that bad. Could be worse."

Beck knew just how bad it could be.

"Did she hurt you?"

"Nah." Tru laughed humorlessly. "She doesn't want to leave any scars that'll show in court."

"Tru—"

"Beck, I'm okay," she said quickly, a little louder. "I can take it. You know I can."

"But you shouldn't have to." Nobody should.

"No, but like you said, it'll be over soon."

This was familiar territory, a kind of game they played.

"And you'll move in with Dad. To your own room," Beck said. "We painted it pink, just for you."

Tru snorted. "Well, you better be painting right over that."

"What?" Beck put on a shocked air. "What about the twinkle lights and glittery letters spelling out your name?"

"I'm sixteen, almost seventeen. Not seven," Tru reminded him with mock severity. Beck could tell she was trying not to laugh, though.

"Don't tell me we'll have to send back the life-sized princess mural."

"Oh, now that I could live with," Tru said, finally giving in to giggles. "Princesses get all the cute guys."

Beck groaned. "Why'd you have to ruin it? I don't need to be thinking about my baby sister as being boy crazy."

"I'm not a baby anymore, Beck."

"Don't remind me."

He heard a muffled sound over the phone before Tru said, "Mommy dearest is up. I better go."

He sat up, concerned. "You sure you're okay?"

"Yeah, of course. Just another day in paradise." She sighed and Beck heard the unmistakable sound of his mother's voice. "Gotta go. Talk to you later, big bro."

Beck warred between trying to keep her on the phone—which he knew would only anger their mother—and dealing with worrying about her once he said goodbye.

"You call me," he told her, choosing the lesser of two evils. "If you get in trouble, you call me, okay? I don't care what the lawyer says. I'll be there in a flash."

"I promise," Tru replied quickly. "Gotta go. Bye, Beck."

"Bye," he said, although she'd already hung up.

Beck lay back, his phone cradled to his chest as he took a deep breath and tried to ease the worry that twisted in his stomach—that was pretty much a constant companion lately, it seemed. He meant what he said, though. If there was a chance of Tru getting hurt, of his mother crossing that line, he would stop at nothing to get his sister away from her, no matter what the courts said.

He fell asleep with the phone clutched in his hand, just in case.

FIVE

Chloe lay curled up on the sofa, wrapped in an afghan as she dozed in fits and spurts. She'd given up sleeping in her room lately. The visions in the window had been coming fast and furious, calling to her multiple times a night on occasion. She found it easier to sleep on the couch—or try to, at least.

She blinked slowly as an image appeared in the glass yet again. It was the same familiar battle scene she'd seen at least a dozen times in the past few days, but she forced herself to sit up and grab the notebook Miranda had left on the coffee table to record any details that might help in their efforts to figure out what was going on.

Or what was *going* to go on at some point in the future.

Chloe yawned and scrubbed at her eyes. "A little more guidance would be greatly appreciated," she muttered to whoever was listening as she took in the scene before her—the wall of black smoke at the edge of the clearing, images of herself, Beck, Wren, a red-haired woman, and a few others she couldn't quite make out racing toward it.

Oh, that was new.

There were others in the clearing. Nobody she recognized from the vantage point of the vision, but at least twenty-five or thirty people, if she was counting correctly. In the darkness and whirling debris, she could barely distinguish the figures running away from the smoke wall.

No, not away from the wall. *Toward* Chloe, Wren and the others. Toward them as if they were going to fight them. As if they were defending the creepy black smoke.

Chloe scribbled frantically in the notebook, but before she could think any more about what she'd seen, the image shifted and she was looking at a dark room, then Beck's face, then that of a younger girl with the same bone structure—high cheekbones and a slightly sharper chin, her skin and hair slightly lighter than Beck's. The sister he'd mentioned, maybe? Then a woman appeared, dark eyes cold and empty as she screamed in anger while Beck raised a glowing hand, his own face twisted in fury as he lunged toward her. Chloe startled at the sudden movement, but just as quickly the image vanished and the window cleared.

She let out a slow breath. "Well, that was decidedly creepy and vague."

The window, as usual, didn't respond, so Chloe put pen to paper and tried to record everything she'd seen.

Beck, apparently, was headed for a bit of a trouble, and she had to make sure he knew it was coming.

"I need you to show me a picture of your sister," Chloe demanded as she cornered Beck at the coffee shop the next day, unceremoniously sliding into the booth next to Wren. It was Saturday, and Chloe had to wait until a reasonable hour to text Wren in an effort to track him down. She'd told him they'd planned to meet and study that afternoon, and Chloe had nearly bitten her nails to the quick as she waited to speak to him.

"Hi, Beck. Nice to see you, Beck. How are you, Beck?" Wren said under her breath, earning a glare from her friend.

"Hi, Beck," Chloe parroted. "Now, I need to see a picture of your sister. Please."

"Why?" he asked, but he pulled out his phone and slid open his photo album.

"I had a vision last night," she replied, hesitantly. "Parts I've seen before, but I couldn't really make sense of them. Now . . ." She examined Beck's face, looking for similarities to the girl she'd seen in the window. "I think she was in it."

Beck froze. "What kind of vision? What happened to Tru?"

Chloe sighed in frustration. "I don't know, exactly. The window isn't always specific. Or sometimes anything beyond vague and frustrating." She huffed and grabbed his hand, angling Beck's phone toward her so she could see the image of Tru, taken on her last birthday, if the candle-filled cake before her was any indication.

"Well?" he prompted.

She nodded. "That's who I saw. And an older woman with enough of a resemblance to guess she's your mother?"

Beck inhaled sharply. "What else?"

Chloe shook her head slightly. "Not much. She was angry, I think. You, too. Your hand was—" she wiggled her fingers and raised her eyebrows. "—you know. And you went after her . . ."

The sounds of clattering silverware and muffled voices filled the silence until Wren said, "And?"

Chloe shrugged. "And nothing. That was it."

Beck watched her closely. "Are you sure about that? What aren't you telling me?"

She sighed and looked up at him. "It's nothing, really," she said. "I mean, that's all I saw. It's just . . ."

"Just?" He resisted the urge to reach out and shake the answer from her.

She swept some crumbs off the table and shook her head slowly. "I didn't see it happen, but I had a feeling —I can't really explain it—that you might have hurt her."

"Who?" Wren asked.

"His mother," she replied, flicking a nervous glance at Beck.

He leaned onto the table on his crossed arms. "I've thought about it a million times," he admitted. "But I can't see myself actually hurting Gina. Not unless . . ." He swallowed, an uneasy, almost nauseated look on his face.

"Unless what?" Chloe asked.

"Unless she hurt Tru," he said, not meeting her eyes. "And if she did that, I don't know that I'd be able to stop myself."

Chloe nodded slowly and they settled into an uneasy silence.

"You've got to get your sister away from her," Wren said quietly. "If she's going to hurt her—"

"We've been trying," Beck answered, trying to control the frustration in his tone. "It's not easy."

"Can't your dad—"

"He's not her biological father," Beck snapped. He caught Wren's startled look. "Sorry," he said. "Tru's

71

bio-dad took off when she was two and we haven't seen or heard from him since. He's not much better than our mom, anyway.

"My dad's been trying to get custody, but it's not easy to take Tru from her biological mother."

Wren reached across the table and grabbed his wrist, her thumb rubbing gently over his skin. He didn't meet her eyes, but he seemed to relax into the touch a bit. Chloe looked away, feeling like she was intruding on a private moment.

"What are you going to do?" Chloe asked once Wren had released him.

Beck shoved away his coffee cup and wiped a hand over his head. "Whatever I have to do to protect my sister," he said. "Although I've got to admit, right now? I have absolutely no idea how to do that."

The potential threat against Tru haunted Beck over the following days. He found himself zoning out during class, during practice, unable to keep from imagining what could happen to his little sister. Vivid thoughts, lurid and terrifying, left him gasping for breath on more than one occasion, his heart pounding with fear. Once he even had to duck behind a bush between classes when he felt a tingle in his hand. The glow was barely there—most people probably wouldn't have noticed it—but he forced himself to count his breaths to calm down and it eventually faded. His burgeoning gift was both exciting and frightening, and he imagined it would continue to be so until he could learn to control it.

So he tried. Every moment he was alone, he worked on accessing the connection to his power, as Wren had taught him. Sitting in his room, late at night, he'd set aside his homework and focus, the glow brightening and fading around his fingers as he worked.

But the strength—the power—it eluded him, the embers barely burning without anger to ignite them. No matter how many times he tried, all he got for his efforts was a glowing hand.

Until he got so fed up and frustrated, he accidentally broke his headboard.

The glow fled quickly, his own shock breaking his concentration and his feelings of anger. With a heavy sigh, he managed to sneak the broken wooden pieces out of the house and into the dumpster.

Obviously, there was something wrong with him. Within a few days, Wren had at least learned to control her gift to some level. Not long after that, she even killed a guy.

Saved a life, too. More than one, actually.

Beck couldn't figure out why he was having so

much difficulty. Why his power seemed so integrally linked to his anger. Why he was so—

Useless. Worthless. Nothing.

The thoughts kept him up at night, the voice reverberating in his skull.

The three of them convened at Chloe's house again on Friday after swim practice, gathering in the attic with two large pizzas on the floor between them. The chest sat in the corner, and Beck couldn't resist glancing at it every now and then.

"Doesn't it give you the creeps?" he asked.

Chloe shrugged. "Not really. I guess I've gotten used to it."

He supposed that made sense.

"Where's Miranda?" Wren asked, wiping her mouth and taking a long swig of her soda. "She has all the notes we're supposed to be reviewing."

"She texted me a little while ago," Chloe replied. "Said she was doing some research, but would be here soon."

"So what do we do until then?" Wren leaned back on her hands and rolled her neck.

"I think you need to help Beck with his power."

"I'm getting better," Beck said, holding up his hand. He concentrated and after only a few seconds it started to glow. "Not that it matters." The glow faded, then brightened again. "All I can do is play human light bulb. I have no control over the strength." His hand faded and he blew out a breath.

"It takes time," Wren said.

"How much time?" Beck snapped. Tru didn't have time. He had to be ready. He had to—

Wren grabbed his wrist. "It takes as long as it takes," she said quietly.

"Well, that's too damn long!" He shook her loose and shot to his feet, his hand glowing brightly. "All I can do is *this*." He clenched his fist, the light so bright it was difficult to look at. "What good is this? How can *this* help anyone?"

Useless. Worthless. Waste of space.

"Beck—" Chloe stood up, holding her hands out in front of her. "You need to calm down."

"That doesn't help either!" he shouted, as he turned and smashed his fist onto the dresser behind him. The wood creaked and groaned before splintering under his hand, splitting in two and collapsing into a pile of battered wood. The attached mirror shattered, glass exploding outward in a spray of shards that caught him along his right side. He flinched at the pain, pinpricks of blood welling up along his exposed skin. A whimpered gasp had him whirling, and he gaped at the sight of Wren and Chloe, both transported to the far side of the attic. A trickle of blood ran down Wren's arm and regret and guilt quickly replaced the rage under Beck's skin.

"Oh my God," he breathed.

Wren wiped the blood away with a finger. "Guess I wasn't quite fast enough."

Beck took a step toward her, and froze when she flinched. "I'm so sorry."

You are sorry. Sorry excuse for a man. Sorry excuse for a son.

He reached out a trembling hand before he dropped it by his side, ashamed. What had he done?

"Beck—" Wren took a step toward him.

"Stay back," he said. "I don't know if I can—I don't want to hurt—I don't—" He felt lightheaded for a moment, unable to do anything but slump to the floor. He sat amidst the dust and shattered glass, his face in his hands, suddenly exhausted.

A warm palm on his head made him shudder and he looked up to find both Chloe and Wren watching him with pity in their eyes.

"I'm so sorry," he whispered.

"It's okay," Wren replied.

He glanced at Chloe. "Are you—"

"I'm fine," she said. "Wren's pretty quick on the draw." She smiled and handed him a wad of napkins. He pressed them to the worst of the cuts and let out a heavy breath.

"I don't know what to do," he said finally. "I can't seem to control this, and I don't want to hurt anyone." His mind immediately flew to his mother. *Almost* anyone.

"We're going to help you," Chloe said.

"But I'm dangerous—"

"You're not." Wren lifted her chin and narrowed her eyes at him. "And even if you were—if you *could be* —you need to be in control of it." She squatted in front of him, her knees almost brushing his. "You know this feeling, right now? The guilt? The fear?"

Beck nodded at the floor, unable to reply through the lump in his throat.

"Just imagine if you *had* really hurt me. Or Chloe." His head whipped up at that, and she continued. "What if you had *killed* one of us. Accidentally. Imagine what that would feel like." Her eyes bore into his, blue and fathomless.

"I know what it feels like to kill someone," she said quietly. "And the only way I can stand it is to keep telling myself that I *had* to do it. That it was the only way and that other lives were on the line."

"Mine, for one," Chloe added.

Wren tipped her head toward Chloe in acknowledgement. "You have to learn to control it," she told Beck. "You *have* to. And we're going to help you."

Beck let out a defeated breath. "I don't know if I can."

"You can," Chloe said firmly. "I've seen it."

Beck looked slowly from one to the other, the determination evident in their shoulders, their unwavering gazes.

"Okay," he said. "Let's do it."

The relief he saw on both of their faces was encouraging, although he still wasn't completely convinced that he wasn't a danger to them. He found he didn't really have any other options, however. He either learned to control the power, or it controlled him. And the only people who could help him learn to do that—if it was even possible—were standing in that attic.

And he had to trust Chloe and her visions. From what he'd learned so far, they had yet to lead her astray.

They took a break to clean up the broken dresser and patch up their cuts and scrapes, then reconvened in the attic. For some reason, it seemed to draw them. Beck wasn't sure what it was about the room, but he felt safer there, isolated from the outside world.

It was nothing he could really explain, but he could sense that Chloe and Wren felt the same way, so he didn't think he was crazy. Well, not any crazier than them, at any rate.

They sat in a circle on the floor, and Beck closed his eyes, breathing slowly.

"Okay," Chloe said. "Go ahead."

Beck nodded and centered his thoughts, focused on his hand. It responded almost immediately and he held it up, the shimmering light encasing it in an iridescent glove.

"That's great," Wren said, scooting toward him. She sat cross-legged before him and reached for his hand, turning it gently as she examined the light surrounding his fingers. "Tell me what you're feeling right now."

Beck tried to ignore the sensation of her touch—a warmth that trickled through him from the points where her fingers gently stroked his. He doubted that was the feeling she was talking about, so he took a deep breath and tried to focus.

"It's a tingling, like you said," he replied. "Kind of a current, I guess—like electricity."

"How are your emotions?" Chloe asked quietly. They'd agreed that she would check in periodically and make sure he wasn't losing it.

"I'm good," he replied. "No anger. Well, not any more than usual, anyway." He shot her a smirk and she smiled back.

Wren shook his hand a little to draw his attention. "Okay, I know this sounds weird, but try and talk to it."

"Talk to it?" He turned a skeptical look on her and she shrugged.

"I don't know how else to say it," she said, releasing his hand. "The electricity—the power—It's part of you, but it's also separate. It'll obey you, or work with you, if you can find a way to communicate with it."

Beck wasn't buying it, but he figured he'd give it a try. "Umm . . . hello?"

Wren snorted. "Not out loud."

The light faded and Beck shook his head, in defeat. "I don't know what you mean," he said. "How do you communicate with a feeling?"

Wren looked dejected. "I don't know how else to explain it. I'm sorry."

Beck got up and scrubbed his hands over his head. "It's not your fault."

"It's not anybody's fault," Chloe interjected. "Maybe we're going about this the wrong way."

"What do you mean?" Wren asked.

Chloe leaned back on her hands. "We've been trying to control his power like you do. But maybe it doesn't work that way for him." She studied Beck for a moment, thinking. "You've been trying to contain your anger, bottle it up, but maybe that's the key to your power. Maybe instead of keeping it away, we need to see if you can learn to focus it."

"Focus it?" Beck looked at his hand, fingers twitching. "Like a weapon? Point and shoot?"

Chloe shrugged. "Worth a shot."

Wren stood up and crossed the attic to dig through some old sports equipment. She held up a worn baseball with a victorious grin. "Here's your first target."

She tossed the ball to Beck, who looked at it skeptically as he caught it. "So, now what?"

Wren crouched next to him. "You know all that anger you have about your mom?"

"Yeah?"

She grabbed the ball and smacked it back into his palm. "Put it right there."

The ball never knew what hit it.

SIX

"Beck, wake up!"

He just about fell out of bed, flailing as his dad burst into his room and crossed to the window, peeking between the blinds. It took a moment for Beck to realize where he was—at his dad's, not Archie Hall. He'd wanted to check on his father and find out if the lawyer had any new information, but after training at Chloe's, he'd been so exhausted, he crashed in his old room instead of heading home.

"What's happening?" he asked as he stumbled to his feet, trying to make sense of the odd, flashing light streaming into the room and the sound of sirens close by.

Too close by.

His father grabbed a sweatshirt off the back of Beck's desk chair and tossed it to him. "Fire next door. We need to evacuate until they get it under control." He kicked a pair of shoes toward him as Beck tugged on the sweatshirt and a pair of jeans, stuffing his phone into his back pocket.

"Fire?" he asked. "At the Jensen's? Are they okay?"

He staggered out of the room behind his dad, running down the stairs with his shoes in his hands. "Is anyone hurt?"

"I don't know." Jacob grabbed a jacket and a small bag that Beck knew contained a laptop and some important papers—birth certificates, social security cards, legal stuff that would be difficult to replace. "The town's gone crazy. Sirens have been going off all night and I thought I heard gunshots earlier." He opened the door and looked back at Beck sternly. "Just stay with me, understand?"

Beck nodded as he slid his feet into his shoes and trailed after his father, gazing up in awe at the house next door engulfed in flames, the heat on his face a counter to the brisk night air behind him. They jogged to the road, where two fire trucks were parked haphazardly, and gathered with a small group of their neighbors, all looking at the burning building. Two groups of firefighters stood, tense and braced against the power of the hoses, shooting water over the flames.

"Stay here. I'm going to see if I can find out anything about the Jensens," his father said before walking over to a firefighter speaking into a walkie-talkie, apparently the guy in charge.

Jamming his hands into his sweatshirt pockets, Beck shivered and blinked the sleep out of his eyes with a yawn. He took a step back and looked around, finally able to focus on the surroundings. The neighborhood was a mess, not even counting the mayhem around the house fire. Garbage cans were upended in the middle of the street, one crunched under the wheel of a black sedan with a dent in the side, parked halfway onto the sidewalk, the driver's side door hanging open and spray paint scrawled across the hood. Paper and trash scattered in the wind, littering front yards up and down the block. Beck could hear another siren, further away, and a distant rumble he realized was shouting.

What in the world was going on?

A man stood in the shadows on the other side of the alley and a rush of awareness tingled up Beck's spine. He wore all black—jeans, jacket and a stocking cap pulled over his ears. In the darkness, Beck couldn't see his eyes, but it still felt like the man was looking in his direction. Staring right at him. Unconsciously, Beck took a step toward him and the man took a step back.

Beck's hand tingled, a surge of adrenaline triggering his gift. He gripped it into a fist, glancing down to make sure the glow wasn't visible through his pocket. It was. Barely. Not enough for anyone else to notice—not with the chaos going on at that moment—but he crossed his other arm over his stomach to hide it, just the same.

The man remained still, legs braced apart, relaxed, but unyielding. A car rounded the corner and headlights illuminated his face for a brief moment, just long enough to give the impression of angular features, middle age, and dark eyes focused on him.

Beck's breath caught. He wasn't imagining it.

He started toward him, but a hand on his arm stopped Beck mid-stride.

"Where are you going?" his dad asked.

Beck opened his mouth to respond, but when he looked back across the street, the man had vanished. He searched the shadows, but could find no sign of him.

"Beck?"

He shook his head. "It's nothing."

Jacob Leighton shrugged. "House is empty. The Jensens aren't home," he said, looking up at the fire. "The house is a loss, though. They're pretty much just trying to keep it from spreading to other buildings at this point."

"Do they know how it started?" Beck asked.

His father frowned. "Bunch of kids, apparently. Maybe gang activity. They're not sure," he said. "They came through, causing trouble . . . vandalizing, looting, that kind of thing. Not sure how they started the fire, though. Not sure why they'd want to. I don't know." He shook his head, brow furrowed as he turned toward the still wailing siren. "It seems like this town's gone crazy or something."

Beck opened his mouth to respond, but his ringing phone interrupted before he could speak. He grabbed it, instantly recognizing his sister's ringtone.

"Tru?"

Only heavy breathing and a soft whimper responded.

"Trulee? Is that you?"

"Guess again," a chillingly familiar voice responded.

Beck's heart stopped. "Gina?"

The woman laughed. "What happened to *Mom*?"

"You lost that privilege a long time ago."

"What's going on?" his father asked. Beck shook his head and held up a finger to hold him off.

"How did I raise such an ungrateful child?" she asked, words slurring. "You're such a disappointment."

"Well, that's nothing new," Beck replied through gritted teeth. "Where's Trulee?"

"Trulee . . . Trulee . . . Truuuuuuleeee . . ." Gina sang tunelessly. "Wouldn't you like to know?"

"What have you done to her?"

"Nothing she didn't deserve," she snapped. "Ungrateful, useless—"

Beck didn't hear the rest of her rant. He hung up the phone and fumbled for his car keys, racing for the house when he realized he'd left them inside.

"Beckett!" His father chased after him, catching him on the way back down the stairs. "What in the world is going on?"

He pushed his way past. "It's Tru. I think she's in trouble."

"Wait, I'll go with you."

"You can't," Beck replied, not slowing his steps. "You know you can't violate the restraining order." He got into his car, only for his father to run around and get in the other side.

"So I'll stay in the car," he said.

"Dad—"

"We don't have time to argue about this," Jacob snapped. "Are you going to drive, or am I going to get my own car?"

Beck let out a frustrated noise and started the car.

"What did Gina say?" Jacob asked.

"The usual," he muttered. "We're ungrateful, miserable children. Tru got what she deserves."

"Jesus." Jacob thumbed at his phone and dialed 911. Beck tried to concentrate on navigating the streets while his father argued with whoever was on the other end of the line. By the time they skidded to a stop in front of Tru's house, he'd hung up in frustration.

"They can't do anything unless we have evidence that some harm's been done to Tru," he said. "The dispatcher said the police have been swamped with calls tonight and they don't have anyone to spare to investigate unless there's real danger."

"Perfect," Beck muttered, slamming the car into park. "Wait here."

"Oh no, you don't," his father replied, grabbing his arm. "There's no way I'm letting you go in there alone."

"Dad, you know you can't go in."

"To hell with the restraining order," he snarled, scrubbing his hand over his face. "They can throw me in jail if they want to."

Beck shook his head slowly. "Dad, no. You know we can't do that. Not if we want Tru permanently," he said. "Let me go in."

His father opened his mouth to protest and Beck hastened to add, "I promise not to do anything crazy. I'll come back out right away, but I have to see if Tru's okay."

After a long moment, he finally nodded. "Okay, but I have my phone on. You call me if Gina tries anything. I mean *anything*."

Beck pressed his lips together. "I will."

The front door was open, and he paused only a moment before walking into the house. It was dark, the only light coming from the kitchen down a long hall-way, and he fought back a feeling of unease.

"Tru? You here?"

A muffled sound drew him toward the back of the house. He padded quietly down the hall, one step after the other—toe first, then heel barely touching as he all but held his breath to keep from being detected.

"Tru?" he whispered. "Tru, are you there?"

"Beck?"

At her quiet voice, fear and worry pushed him forward, eliminating any hope of stealth. Beck raced into the kitchen, and found her huddled in the corner near the refrigerator, eyes wide and frightened. He fell to his knees before her and ran his hands over her arms searching for injuries.

"Are you hurt? What is it?"

With a quiet cry she lunged forward, wrapping him in a tight hug. "I'm so glad you're here."

He stroked her back gently. "Tru, you've gotta tell me what's going on," he pleaded. "Where's Gina?"

"I don't know," she whispered. "She . . . I don't—" She broke off in a quiet sob.

Beck squeezed her tightly once, then pulled back. "I'm getting you out of here. Come on." He helped her up, keeping his arm protectively around her shoulders.

They shuffled toward the hall, only to stop short at the sight of the dark figure looming there.

"Where do you think you're going?" Gina asked, swaying slightly on her feet.

Beck hesitated only for a moment, but pushed his sister behind him. "I'm taking Tru and we're leaving."

Gina laughed harshly. "Nope, you're not. She's mine. She stays."

"No. She doesn't."

Gina stared at him, her grin maniacal and unsettling in the dim light. She stepped forward out of the shadows and Beck heard Tru's sharp inhale echo his own.

What the . . .

Even at her worst, Gina had never looked so unkempt, her clothes mismatched and dirty, her hair slipping haphazardly out of her usual neat braids in matted clumps. She spun her wedding ring around her finger slowly, methodically.

"What's wrong with you?" he murmured. "Your eyes . . ."

Her eyes looked black at first glance, but as she took another step closer, Beck realized the darkness moved—swirling like smoke between her lids. He couldn't keep from staring as an uneasy chill ran up his spine.

"Beck?" Tru said in a trembling voice.

He squeezed her hand. "It's okay. We're getting out of here."

Beck tugged her forward, ready to push by Gina if he had to, but his mother's wild smile only widened, the eerie smoke drifting out between her teeth, and she reached out in a flash to grab his wrist, fingernails digging into his skin as she pulled him close with unexpected strength.

He froze under her stare, mesmerized by the pulsing blackness as she seemed to look right through him. Her grip tightened and he looked down, stunned to see more of the smoke spiraling out from her fingers to wrap around his bare forearm.

"What—" He choked as she blew a stream of smoke into his mouth. Beck coughed against the acrid taste, barely aware of Tru whimpering behind him.

"Just let it happen," Gina said quietly, her grin fading as she leaned in to speak to him fervently. "It's good, isn't it? All that anger. It makes you strong."

Beck couldn't look away from her eyes, the black pits seeming to grow deeper the longer he stared. He was vaguely aware of tingling in his fingertips and in the back of his mind, he knew that if he looked down, his hand would be glowing.

He couldn't though. Look down. All he could do was stare into his mother's bottomless eyes as he felt the anger course through him. The woman before him was evil personified— degradation and humiliation. Shame.

She was why Beck and Tru didn't have friends over

when they were little—too many times she'd stumbled into the room after one too many glasses of wine.

She was full of excuses when they were forgotten after school. She was screaming fights with Beck's father, and later, Tru's. She was frustration and anxiety. She was that voice in the back of Beck's head that told him he wasn't good enough. Strong enough. Anything enough.

She was fury. Fear. Hate.

And she rushed through his veins, pulsing with every breath in and out.

"That's right," she choked out, and Beck realized he had wrapped his hand around her throat, his glowing fingers lifting her up onto her toes.

"You know you want to," she said, barely able to get the words out. "Remember all those times I said you were stupid? Worthless? I deserve this, right?"

She did. She deserved it all and more. He lifted her higher, grinning when she gasped for air, no longer able to form words as her feet dangled off the floor.

"Beck, stop!" Tru hung from his arm and he shook her off without effort. Power coursed through him. Strength. He could do anything. He could finally stop Gina. He could do whatever he wanted.

"Beckett!" When had his father come into the room? "What's wrong with him?" he asked Tru. It didn't matter. Jacob couldn't stop him. Nobody could.

Beck was . . . he was *everything*.

Beck felt hands on his cheeks. Heard someone calling his name from a distance, but it didn't matter. None of it mattered. All that he cared about was ending Gina, for once and for all.

Then . . .

Then, he didn't know.

You can have whatever you want.

That's right. He could. He could have anything.

Power. Wealth. Revenge.

"Beck? Beck, it's Wren. Can you hear me?"

Wren? What was she doing there?

You can have her, too. Just take what you want.

"Wren, you have to do it."

"I don't know if I can."

"Try. You have to try. Be careful, though. He's really strong."

Gina's eyes rolled back. Beck smiled and tightened his grip. Then, there was a flash of light and everything changed.

"Beck. Beck, look at me. Please."

He blinked and turned away from Gina to find Wren searching his eyes, her own wet as she stroked his cheeks.

"That's right. Listen to my voice," she said.

Don't listen to her. Finish it.

"Wren?"

She smiled gently. "Yeah, it's me. I knew you were in there somewhere."

"What?"

"Beck. You need to let go of Gina. You're going to kill her."

She deserves to die.

"She deserves to die." Did Beck say that? Or someone . . . else? It seemed like there was someone else.

"No. No, Beck." Wren squeezed his face slightly, her fingertips digging into his cheeks. "No, you can't do that. It doesn't matter what she did. It's not right. You have to stop."

"Stop?" He loosened his fingers a little.

"Yeah, that's right. Let her go. You have to let her go."

You don't have to do anything.

"Beck, this isn't you. Look around. Look at what you've done."

Beck blinked and looked beyond her shoulder to where Tru lay slumped against the wall, a streak of blood on her temple. His father knelt next to her, and Chloe had a hand on his arm, as if supporting him, although they all were frozen in place.

"What? What happened?"

It doesn't matter. None of them matter.

"Shut up!" he shouted. "Stop talking to me!"

"Beck?" Wren's hands were stroking his cheeks again. "Beck, it's okay. You can fight it."

I can give you everything you want.

"No! Leave me alone!" Beck squeezed his eyes shut and shook his head violently. "No!"

You don't want that. I'm part of you now. We're one. We're the same. We—

"We're not the same," Beck all but snarled, releasing Gina as he opened his eyes and took a stumbling step back. He inhaled sharply through his nose and tried to calm his racing heart. "We're not the same." He stood, legs braced apart as he focused on a churning feeling deep inside him. The anger and hate he'd fanned into a flame. He pictured it, a black pulsing mass in the depths of his gut.

"Get. *Out.*"

His right hand flew forward, the glowing glove brighter than ever, nearly blinding as the light pulsed along his skin. He squinted as black smoke poured from his fingertips, winding its way back toward Gina, who he just realized was suspended six inches off the ground.

Beck let out a breath as the last of the darkness left him, curling around Gina's head before disappearing, sucked into her open mouth. He turned to Wren with a questioning look.

She was holding his upper arm, watching him carefully. "Are you okay?"

He nodded, suddenly exhausted. "I take it you're the reason we're the only ones that seem to be moving at the moment."

She smiled softly. "Stopped time for both of us. Wasn't sure if it'd work, to be honest, but we had to try something to get through to you."

He flexed his glowing fingers, the strength still pulsing through him. "I could have hurt you."

"You wouldn't have."

"You don't know that."

She slid her fingers between his, the light wrapping around both of them. "Yeah, I do."

He drew in a shaky breath and looked back at Gina, frozen in place and still hovering in mid-air. "What do we do now?"

Wren squeezed his hand and closed her eyes. Like restarting a paused movie, action around them slowly started up again as Gina floated toward the floor, and landed with a thump as time resumed.

It wasn't until then that Beck realized how silent everything had been—as the voices and sobs and even the squeak of the swinging front door drifted toward him. Tru let out a pained moan, jolting Beck into action and he rushed across the room, falling to his knees before her.

"Tru? Tru, are you okay? Oh, God, I'm so sorry. Please be okay." It wasn't until he reached out to touch her that he realized his hand had stopped glowing.

"Beck?" Tru touched her head and blinked at the blood that came away on her fingertips. "What happened?"

"Try not to move," Chloe cautioned. "Maybe we should call an ambulance?"

"No, no." Tru started to get up, tugging on Beck's arm for balance. "I'm okay. I just want to get out of here and away from—" She froze, looking over Beck's shoulder. "Where's Mom?"

Beck and the others turned toward where Gina had collapsed on the floor.

But the front door was open. And Gina was gone.

SEVEN

"Beck? Beck, wake up. Someone's here." Tru shoved on his shoulder and he rolled over, pulling his pillow over his face.

"Tell them to go away."

"It's two in the afternoon. You've been sleeping forever!"

"Just five more minutes," he mumbled.

Tru's voice took on that sing-songy, teasing lilt that had Beck wondering why he ever wanted his sister to live under the same roof with him. "But it's your girl-friend . . ." She bounced on the bed a couple times. "Okay, if you really want me to tell her to go away . . ." Tru started to get up, but Beck reached out and grabbed her arm to stop her.

"Shut up," he muttered when she started to laugh.

He rolled out of bed and couldn't keep the small smile off his face when Tru bumped his hip with her own. A Band-Aid on her forehead was the only remnant of her injury from the night before. His eyes went straight to it and a wave of guilt nearly took his breath away. He opened his mouth to apologize—again —but Tru punched him in the shoulder.

"Stop it," she snapped. "It wasn't your fault, so stop feeling bad."

"But I'm—"

"I said, stop it." She hugged him briefly before heading for the door. "Hurry up. She's waiting."

In the end, they had called the police to report Gina, but the cops hadn't been able to turn up any sign of her. She'd disappeared without a trace—no car, no witnesses, no indication that she'd used a credit card or ATM that night.

Beck didn't really care, to be honest. He was counting his blessings. With Gina out of the picture, his dad was the next of kin, and he could only hope that Gina stayed gone and Tru stayed with him. He'd returned to his dad's house the night before, barely able to let Tru out of his sight. It had felt right with her sleeping just down the hall, in the room they'd readied for her, and he wondered if he'd ever be able to return to Archie Hall.

He stumbled down the stairs, rubbing his eyes, with Tru close on his heels. She flew out the door, saying she was heading over to a friend's house, apparently none the worse for wear, despite the night's events. She'd been unconscious for most of the more supernatural happenings, and a little out of it for the rest, and his father had been too focused on her injuries to notice Beck's glowing hand or the weird black smoke. In his mind—and in Tru's, for that matter—it had been just another time Tru's mother had hurt her. It was sad, really, that it wasn't that unusual for her, and Tru's resiliency had come at a price over the years.

But she would be okay. Beck would make sure of it.

He yawned and walked into the kitchen. To his surprise, Wren wasn't alone. Chloe, Ethan, and Miranda sat around the table, looking up at him expectantly.

"Don't you people ever sleep?" he asked, yanking open the fridge door to grab some orange juice.

"It's Miranda's fault," Chloe said with a yawn, but she smiled at her friend's offended gasp.

"It's not my *fault*," she said. "I just thought that we needed to get all of this new information down while it was fresh in our minds." She whipped out a laptop from somewhere and started tapping at the keys.

"How'd you even find me?" Beck took a gulp of juice, then rolled his eyes as Chloe gave him a wry look. "Oh yeah, right," he said, wiping his mouth with the back of his hand. "I guess I have to get used to psychic friends knowing where I am at any given moment."

"I'm not psychic," Chloe said, in the voice of one who's made the argument many times before.

"Psychic-*ish*," Miranda muttered in the same tone.

"Anyway," Wren said, drawing out the word. "Is Tru okay?"

Beck looked toward the door where he'd last seen her. He still dealt with the worry, but knew there was only so much he could do to protect her. "She's okay," he said quietly. "Resilient, you know?"

"How about you?" Ethan asked.

Beck shrugged. He didn't even know the answer to that question.

"It wasn't your fault," Wren said.

"Sure feels like it."

"But it's not," Ethan said. "I get it. I don't remember much, but that—the feeling. I don't know if I could have stopped if it hadn't left me."

"Which begs the question . . . why," Miranda said, typing on her computer. "It left you, but Beck had to fight it off—push it out."

"So they were what? Possessed?" Wren asked.

"No," Beck said, clearing his throat and taking a sip of juice. "Not possessed. Not really." In the ensuing silence, he eyed everyone watching him closely. "It's not like I wasn't in control. It's like he—*it*—convinced me to do what it wanted. I believed what it was telling me."

"Interesting," Miranda murmured, fingers flying over the keys while she recorded his comments.

"That's one way to put it," Beck replied flatly as he put the juice back and dragged another chair over to the table. "Creepy. Invasive. Horrifying. Those might be the words I'd choose." He felt fingers intertwine with his and glanced over to see Wren watching him, eyes wide and sad.

"I'm sorry," she whispered.

Beck squeezed her hand in reassurance. "It was like I was two people." He tried to find the right words to explain what had happened. "One was watching it all. Detached almost. The other—" He shook his head.

"See, and I hardly remember anything at all," Ethan said quietly, eyes narrowed as he tried to focus. "It's almost like it was toying with me, and then gave up. Turned its attention elsewhere."

"Like it wanted to *use* you," Wren said. "But it wanted to *take* Beck."

Beck shuddered. That's exactly what it felt like.

Chloe cleared her throat. "I know this is hard," she said. "But like Ethan said, he doesn't remember much, so you're basically the only one with first-hand knowledge of what we're dealing with here. It was *inside* you, but you were able to *resist* it somehow. It's the first indication that this thing—whatever it is—has a weakness, or can maybe even be defeated."

"I don't know what to tell you," Beck replied. "It's all such a blur. It—" He ran his free hand over his head, scratching lightly. "It played off my own emotions—fear, hate, anger," he said slowly, remembering the turmoil he'd felt. How it had settled once he started listening to the voice—*believing* it. "It can't—I don't think it can *make* you do anything. It just convinces you that you *want* to do it, if that makes sense.

"It's like it feeds off the hate or something," he said, eyes narrowing as he concentrated on what he'd felt as he held Gina by the throat. "It makes it stronger. Gives it power."

"Do you know what it is?" Wren asked.

Beck blinked and took a deep breath, shaking his head as he searched for the answer. He could only come up with one word that seemed to fit.

"Chaos," he said.

Fifty miles away in the corner unit of a cheap motel, Gina and the chaos inside her sat and looked out a window at the pouring rain. She sipped lukewarm coffee and idly spun her ring around her finger as she waited for further instructions.

She knew she had failed. Wondered what her punishment would be. Half expected to die at any moment.

And couldn't seem to amass even a shred of emotion about that. No fear. No remorse. Nothing.

"I'm sorry," she whispered.

A heavy sigh resounded inside her, and she could feel it vibrating against her bones from head to toe.

"You failed me," It said.

"I know."

"Don't do it again."

She felt the power tingling under her skin and let out a breath, relieved It hadn't abandoned her. She took another sip of coffee and smiled.

"I won't."

"I found something." Miranda slid into a booth at the coffee shop with the others a week later, carefully setting her open laptop before her. It had become a bit of a habit to meet up in the early evenings to discuss Chloe's visions, Miranda's research, and any other odd happenings around town.

Which seemed to be increasing—fights, vandalism,

fires. At the moment, it seemed to be focused on the downtown area and hadn't filtered out to the campus much, but they all agreed that it was only a matter of time. Especially if Chloe's visions were right, which so far, they seemed to be.

Beck scooted a little closer to Wren to make room, and smiled when she leaned into the touch. Across the table, Ethan and Chloe sat up a little straighter at Miranda's words.

"Found something about what?" Beck asked.

Miranda's fingers flew over the keyboard. "I took a picture of that symbol on the chest," she replied. "I wasn't able to find anything on an Internet search, so I posted it in a couple of online forums—history, mythology geeks, that kind of thing." She stopped with a smug smile and spun the laptop around toward them. "Voila!"

Taking up half the screen was a grainy image of an old book, faded brown-leather maybe, with what appeared to be a metal seal in the center. The design on the seal—

"That's the symbol on the chest," Chloe murmured, reaching out to touch the screen and run her fingers along the intersecting spirals.

"Exactly," Miranda said with a grin. "And there's more. My cousin, Maia, is an anthropology major over at the Seattle campus of WA U. I sent the picture of the book over to her and she found a copy of it on microfilm in the library's special collections."

"Well, don't keep us in suspense," Wren said, her knee jiggling against Beck's. "What is it? What did it say?"

Miranda visibly deflated. "Not much. It's in some ancient language so she has to talk to her professor and try and find someone who can translate it. She did say it seems to be a record of something called The Order."

"What could that be?" Beck asked, not expecting an answer.

Miranda shrugged. "No idea. But get this, Maia just *happen*ed to transfer to the Anthro department *here* to work on her thesis. She's been here since the beginning of the semester and I had no idea."

"Well, isn't that a coincidence," Wren said.

"Right." Ethan scoffed. "I don't think there is such a thing anymore."

"She said I can come meet her tomorrow after class and take a look." She looked around the table loftily. "Of course, if anyone would care to join me . . ."

Chloe laughed. "Like you could stop me."

"If you're going, I'm going," Ethan said, dropping an arm over her shoulder. "Anything to finally get some answers about all of this."

Beck nodded. "Me, too."

"Well, that settles that." Wren lifted her coffee in a mock toast. "Looks like we're all going."

They tapped their cups together. Tomorrow couldn't come soon enough.

———

They met at the coffee shop the next afternoon and gathered around a table while they waited for Wren to finish her shift. They chatted about unimportant things, but Beck could feel the tension. Knew—like the others did—that they were finally on the verge of getting some answers about everything that had been going on. He wasn't sure, however, that they'd like what they found out.

It was like the world was speeding up around them, hurtling toward an inevitable conclusion that they were in no way prepared for. But *maybe* Miranda's cousin could help them at least learn what they were dealing with. Or how they might come out of all this alive.

"How did I not know you had a cousin at WA U?" Chloe asked quietly, eyeing Miranda across the table.

Miranda gulped down the last of her latte before answering. "She grew up in Wisconsin," she said. "I'd only met her a couple times myself before she moved to Seattle to go to school. She's been over to my house for long weekends—Thanksgiving, too—but I guess you guys never crossed paths."

Chloe nodded. "It's just . . . It kind of messes with your mind, you know? With everything going on, and you just happened to have a cousin who's studying at a nearby university who just happens to have access to this mysterious book." She chewed on her lip, looking out the window.

Beck cleared his throat. "It's like we're all puppets. And someone else is pulling the strings."

Chloe glanced at him. "Yeah. Not sure I like the feeling."

"Can I get you guys anything else?" The barista, Dylan, appeared at the table and started to stack up the empty cups and plates.

Miranda handed him her cup and they both fumbled it, Dylan barely managing to catch it before it hit the table. Pink-cheeked and wide-eyed, they exchanged *sorries* and for a moment, Beck relished in the normality of it.

So much of his life was anything but normal lately.

Dylan backed away and a few minutes later Wren approached, yanking her jacket on. "You guys ready for this?"

Were they? Beck wasn't sure. But he also knew there was no looking back.

They walked in silence to the campus as the sun

slipped below the horizon and passed the library, the distant sound of Friday night dorm parties mingling with the hum of streetlights. Miranda led the way, texting her cousin when they came close to a large brick building, and she bounced up the steps just as a tall redhead swung open one of the glass doors and waved.

Chloe stopped in her tracks at the bottom of the stairs.

"What is it?" Ethan asked, glancing up to where Miranda was hugging the girl tightly, then back at Chloe.

"I've seen her before," she replied.

"I thought you said you'd never met," Beck said as he, Wren, and Ethan formed a semi-circle around her.

"We haven't."

It took a moment for Beck to catch on—longer than either Wren or Ethan, if their sharp inhales were any indication.

"You mean, you *saw* her," he said finally, "in the window."

Chloe nodded. "She's there. In the field when we fight."

"She's one of us." Wren sighed and nudged Beck's arm with her own. "Another puppet?"

Beck sighed, but didn't respond. What was there to say?

"Hey, you guys coming?" Miranda called from the top of the steps.

They started forward and Ethan asked Chloe in a low voice, "Are you going to tell her?"

"I kind of have to, don't I?"

Beck held Wren back as the others climbed the stairs. When she looked at him questioningly he felt his cheeks heat and gazed down at his feet, his palm going sweaty where he held her hand.

"I just realized I never thanked you," he said. "You know, for bringing me back. For keeping me from hurting Gina."

"You don't have to thank me."

He looked up, his nerves eased a bit by the warmth in her eyes. "Yeah, I do. I think . . . I think I would have killed her, Wren. If you hadn't been there—"

She squeezed his hand and took a step closer. "I *was* there, so there's no point thinking about what might have been. It's over now. You fought it off."

"Well, I couldn't have done it without you."

Wren huffed out a quiet laugh. "That settles it then. We're both awesome."

Beck shook his head and grinned. "Yeah, we kind of are." This time, he squeezed her hand. "Especially you."

Wren blushed, her pale skin going pink and he reached up to touch her cheek, mesmerized for a moment at the contrast between his skin and hers—dark and light, rough and so, so soft.

He leaned in, his gaze locking on her wide, blue eyes. Her breath caught as his lips brushed against hers and he took that as permission to deepen the kiss. His fingers slid around the nape of her neck and he felt Wren's fists curl into the sides of his t-shirt, her breath soft against his mouth as they broke apart, only to come together once again.

"Hey!"

They jumped at the sound of Ethan's shout, blushing and short of breath but smiling widely when their eyes met.

"You guys going to make out all day or do you plan to join us at some point?" he called from the top of the stairs.

"Yeah, yeah, we're coming!" Beck shouted back as he grabbed Wren's hand and the two of them headed toward the door.

Ethan grinned and went back inside, letting the door slam shut behind him.

"Well, that was embarrassing," Wren muttered as they climbed the stairs.

Beck shrugged as he held the door for her. "To be honest, it doesn't bother me to be caught kissing a pretty girl."

She blushed again and Beck smiled. He thought

making Wren blush could quickly become his new favorite pastime.

Well, and kissing her. That was probably his favorite, but the blush thing came in a close second.

"Besides—" he said, then stopped short as a sudden shiver ran down his spine. He whirled around in the doorway, scanning the darkening shadows, the unmistakable feeling of being watched triggering his nerves.

A rustle off to his left caught his attention and he saw a woman lurking near a group of trees. She smiled slowly, the streetlights reflecting off her dark eyes.

Gina.

"Beck?"

He jumped and turned to find Wren watching him, a worried look on her face. "You okay?"

"It's—" He pointed toward the trees with a trembling finger. But Gina was gone.

"What is it?" she asked.

"I thought—" He took a step back outside, the door swinging shut behind him. Beck searched the surrounding area, eyes darting from shadow to shadow, but he saw no sign of his mother. "It was Gina. I swear, I just saw her."

"*Here?*" Wren took his hand, looking around nervously. "Are you sure?"

"Yeah. Yeah, I am," he replied. "She's gone now, but I have a feeling it's not for long."

Wren squeezed his hand and shivered slightly as she took one more sweeping look at the trees. "Are you okay?"

He nodded. "Yeah, I'm good."

She tugged on his hand. "Come on. Let's go join the others. Maybe we'll finally get some answers that will tell us how to deal with her—or whatever it is that's inside her."

"Maybe." Beck pulled the door open for Wren and took one last look around before following her inside. He hoped Wren was right. Because he knew first-hand what the thing was inside his mother.

And he knew that defeating it was going to be next to impossible.

Gina Talbot had slipped into the shadows, but her eyes remained on the building before her—tall, brick, and stately as were all the buildings scattered on the college campus. Her son and the others disappeared inside, but still she stood, waiting for something.

Waiting for instructions.

She could feel It inside her, twisting with rage, and she didn't dare voice her questions . . . didn't dare move.

She'd learned her lesson. It was best to wait, to be

patient. The alternative could be painful, to say the least.

"Let's go," It whispered at last.

She turned and followed the sound of distant sirens, the potential for delicious violence a potent lure to the thing dwelling inside her.

EIGHT

Something was strange.

Maia Sheridan couldn't put her finger on what caused the odd sense of déjà vu that accompanied the arrival of her cousin, Miranda, and her friends. She'd met them at the door to the Anthro building and pulled Miranda into a quick hug, but couldn't shake that unsettling feeling.

"I didn't realize this was a party," she'd said, eyeing the group at the bottom of the stairs.

Her cousin laughed. "Well, it's a group project so I, uh, brought the group along." She didn't meet Maia's eyes for some reason, giving the impression it might not have been the whole story, but Maia didn't have time to pursue the issue before Miranda pointed behind her at a pretty blonde, then a petite, dark-haired girl.

"The tall one's Wren. Then that's Chloe, Ethan and Beck." She gestured at two tall, muscular guys— one blond, the other dark-skinned with a shaved head.

Miranda raised her voice, calling toward them. "Hey, you guys coming?"

They nodded and started up the stairs, and for some reason, Maia couldn't take her eyes off Chloe. There was something familiar about her. Miranda had mentioned Chloe in the past—they were best friends after all—but Maia had never met her personally.

And yet, there was something about her . . .

"You okay?" Miranda asked, squeezing her elbow.

"Yeah, sure." Maia started, shaking her head and blowing a red curl out of her eyes. "Well, come on. I'm all set up for you guys."

The group followed Maia through the quiet hall—the building was all but empty with Christmas break starting in a few days—to a narrow stairway in the back. They went down two flights to the basement, and it was like going back several decades. Where the school's main library had been updated over the years with comfortable chairs, warm lighting and the latest technology, the Anthro and History research department in the basement was a mess of microfiche, old newspapers, drawers crammed full of historical documents nobody had time to digitize, and in a small room in the northeast corner, the so-called special collections section. It was Maia's favorite place to be, the shelves along three walls lined with copies of ancient texts—a few originals even. It was like a secret haven, dedicated to the past, the only nod to the present was a small research center in the corner comprised of a laptop, combination printer/scanner, and another microfiche projector.

They walked into the room and Maia noticed Ethan and Beck—she wasn't sure which was which yet —stayed by the door, almost like they were standing guard.

Weird.

"I went ahead and printed out a couple copies so we wouldn't have to use the fiche," she told the group, pointing to the stack of paper on the table in the center of the room. "It'll be a lot easier to read."

Miranda picked up a copy. "I don't know about that," she said, flipping through the pages. "I can't read any of this."

Chloe nudged Miranda in the shoulder as she smiled at Maia. "What she means, of course, is that we so appreciate you helping us out."

Maia returned the girl's smile, but still couldn't shake that weird feeling. "Have we met before?"

Chloe glanced toward the door before answering. "No, I don't think so."

"I swear you look familiar or something."

"You've probably just heard a lot about me," she said, but she chewed on her lip nervously. "You know, from Miranda." She glanced at Miranda, and there was . . . *something* in her gaze.

"Yeah, yeah," said Miranda. "That's probably it."

"I think you should just tell her," the blond guy at the door said with a sigh.

"Ethan . . ." Chloe scrubbed at her face.

Well, at least now Maia knew which guy was which.

"Tell me what?" she asked. "What's going on?"

The next few seconds would have been comical if they weren't also very confusing. Chloe glared at Ethan. He glared back, and she turned to Beck, who shrugged. Wren stepped forward and patted Chloe's shoulder gently as she raised her eyebrows at her. It was like a silent conversation was going on between everyone in the room but Maia.

In the end, they all looked toward Miranda, who let out a groan and slumped into a seat.

"Why does almost everybody I know have superpowers . . . except me?" she asked, throwing her hands up. "It's getting really annoying."

Maia huffed out an astonished laugh. "What? What are you even talking about?"

Miranda waved a hand toward Chloe, who swallowed uncomfortably.

"Well," she said, "I . . . I think after you tell us what you found in the book, maybe I'll be able to explain?"

Maia noticed nobody would meet her eyes. They were all watching Chloe.

"Okay," Maia said slowly. "Like I told Miranda, I have to get some help translating it, but I was able to make out a few things." She reached for a packet and flipped through it. "Here on page six, for example, there's a reference to this group, The Order—I highlighted it. The name pops up numerous times through the text. From what I can discern, this book is a record of this group. A journal of some kind."

The others crowded around the table, looking at the highlighted pages.

"What else could you read?" Chloe asked, running her fingers along the margin.

"Well, it's only because I'm in an intro to world religions course, but I recognized a few names. Juracán, a Taíno deity. Set, an ancient Egyptian god. Eris from Greek mythology. But what's interesting is that they all seem to interact with this Order."

"Okay, you've lost me," Ethan said. "So, you're talking about mythological gods?"

"It's not just that," Maia replied, warming to her subject. "These are gods from different cultures, different parts of the world, but they all have something in common. They are all gods of chaos."

"Chaos." Chloe glanced at Beck.

"Chaos, strife, discord, anarchy." Maia paced back

and forth in front of the group. "Whatever you call it, that's what these deities represent. And from what I can tell, they're all somehow linked to this Order."

Maia looked around the group, surprised at the mix of panic and fear on their faces.

She laughed. "Relax, guys. It's all just myths. It'll sure make an interesting project, though. I'd love to get in on it."

For some reason, Miranda choked on a laugh, but before Maia could find out why, Wren asked, "What language is this, anyway?"

"That's the really weird thing," Maia said, the excitement of discovery evident in her voice. "The text covers centuries and it's written in at least six different languages. It's like it was . . . I don't know, passed on or something from scribe to scribe. I mean, it's not the original copy of some of the older records, but there are notations from ancient Mesopotamia, dating this group —The Order—back to the fourth millennium BCE.

"It's incredibly interesting. I can't wait to get the rest translated. But if The Order existed that long ago —and still *does* exist in some form—this could be the Templars or the Masons times a hundred. This could give us insight into mythologies that we haven't seen before. I might write my own pap—"

"Umm," Miranda raised a hand to cut her off. "I get that this gets your scientist-y mind all worked up, but I need to back up a second. You think The Order still exists?"

"Well, it would be difficult to know for sure until the whole text is translated, but secret societies like this, they don't just disappear." She leaned forward on the table and tapped a finger on the paper. "I mean, according to this journal, it's been around for centuries—*millennia*—I can't imagine it would die out."

The screech of wood on linoleum drew their attention to the head of the table, as Ethan pulled out a chair and motioned to the others to do the same.

"This could take a while," he said with a shrug. "We might as well get comfortable." He shot a pointed look toward Chloe, who let out a heavy sigh as she sat down.

"Okay," she said, "I guess there are a few things you should know."

That odd feeling of déjà vu? It was still there. Along with disbelief, confusion, and a heavy dose of anger. Oh, and fear. Definitely some fear mixed in there, too.

"Is this some kind of joke?" Maia asked, shoving her chair back as she stood up. She'd sat there quietly, listening to Chloe talk. She kept her mouth closed when she wanted to speak and Miranda touched her arm to silence her. But *this*? This was just too much.

"Maia, just listen to what they have to say," Miranda said quietly.

"I *have* been listening," she snapped. "I listened to all of it. Every ridiculous word." She pointed at Chloe. "You see the future. There's a magical chest in your attic that gives out powers like a supernatural vending machine." Then to Wren and Beck. "You freeze time and you're super strong." Her finger landed on Ethan. "And you—"

He held up his hands defensively. "I'm just moral support. And a little extra muscle when needed."

Maia let out a frustrated sound. "You guys, I don't have time for this . . ." She waved a hand around, ". . . whatever this is. I volunteered to help you out, but I have my own stuff to do. So if you don't mind—"

"You've got to show her," Ethan said in a low voice. "It's the only way."

"Show me what?"

Chloe nodded at Beck, who held up his hand. As Maia watched, it started to glow—a bright glove of light shimmering around his fingers. She gasped, then started when Wren appeared behind her right shoulder, smiling gently.

"But how—" Before she could finish the question, Wren had vanished again and was back in her seat before Maia could even blink. Beck smirked at her, wiggling his glowing fingers, and Chloe watched her carefully, waiting for a response.

So Maia gave her one.

She shot to her feet, ripped open the door, and ran.

After about fifteen minutes of wandering around campus in a daze, Maia realized what she had done. No, not that she had run away from a group of what was either a bunch of potentially crazy people or an elaborate cruel prank. But she had left the special collections room open and unlocked; the key she'd checked out at the reference desk was still deep in her pocket.

She did not need this on her permanent record. If such a thing existed, and she was pretty certain—given her luck—that it did.

So she did what any mature adult would do. She hid in the bushes outside the Anthro building until she saw Miranda and her friends leave, then went inside, stuffed the remaining copy of The Order book into her backpack and locked up before heading to her dorm.

Her heart still pounded, adrenaline making her hands shake, as she fumbled with her room key and spared one quick look over her shoulder before going inside. Her roommate, Tessa, lay sprawled on her bed —books, papers and laptop haphazardly spread about her.

"One more final," she grumbled. "One more final and it's on a Friday. What kind of person schedules a Chem final on a Fr—" She looked up and her dark, almond shaped eyes narrowed in concern. She swept her long, black hair into a ponytail and slipped off the bed in one graceful movement.

"What's wrong? You're white as a ghost."

"So what else is new?" Maia said, glancing at her pale, freckled face in the mirror.

Tessa snorted. "Shut up. You know what I mean. What happened?"

"It's nothing, I just—" Maia yanked open her closet door and shook her hands to stop the trembling. "I'm fine." She stepped behind the door to change into a pair of yoga pants and her cuddliest sweatshirt.

"Yeah, right," Tessa said, shutting the closet when Maia emerged. "What's got you so upset?"

Maia sighed. How was she supposed to answer that question? In fact, at that moment, she had no idea why she was so freaked out. Sure, the whole vanishing girl trick was unnerving, but it was just that—a trick—and she'd let herself be taken in by it. She felt kind of ridiculous now. Angry. Confused. Unsure of what Miranda and her friends were really trying to do. But she didn't want to get into all of that with Tessa. All she wanted to do was forget about it.

She collapsed onto her bed and rolled onto her stomach, tucking her pillow beneath her. "I just thought maybe someone was following me," she said, forcing a weak smile when Tessa stiffened. "He wasn't. He turned and went the other way before I got close to the dorm, but I got myself all worked up." She closed her eyes and inhaled deeply. "I overreacted. It's nothing, really."

"You sure?"

"Yeah. Absolutely." Maia grabbed the stack of mail she hadn't had time to deal with yet, frowning when she saw an envelope from the University's Housing and Residence Living department. She tore it open, her heart sinking when she read the contents.

"What is it?" Tessa asked.

Maia tossed the letter toward her. "Apparently, after Christmas break, I'm homeless."

"What?" Tessa scanned the letter. "I don't get it. I thought you had that single reserved for when I leave." Tessa's mom was sick, so she'd be transferring to a school back in Wisconsin to be closer to her family. Instead of dealing with another new roommate, Maia had put in a request for a single room.

"I did." She groaned. "But now it looks like that's not going to happen."

Tessa continued reading the letter. "And this room has already been assigned."

"Yep."

"And there's no other room available in this dorm." She flipped over the page. "In *any* dorm."

"Nope."

"So all you can do is get on a waiting list?"

"Or find an apartment." Maia threw an arm over her arms, not wanting to deal with any of it. "I guess it's time to start scanning Craigslist."

"Crap, I'm sorry Maia. I didn't mean to leave you in a bind."

"It's not your fault," she replied. "Don't worry about it. I'll figure it out."

After a while, Tessa returned to her homework, flipping a few pages idly, before she shut the book.

"You hungry?"

Maia shrugged, but didn't open her eyes. "I could eat."

"Dining Hall?"

The thought of going out again made her cringe, but she tried not to show it. "Ugh. Mystery meat? No thanks."

Tessa hummed in thought. "Pizza?" she picked up her phone, waving it with a grin.

Maia sat up, eager to forget the day's events in a haze of cheese and pepperoni.

"Now you're talking."

Maia didn't speak to Miranda for a couple days, but as Christmas break drew closer by the hour, she found herself wondering what she could do. She couldn't afford to fly home, and the letter from Housing said she had to vacate her dorm room by the time they closed for the holidays. She'd tried to plead her case with the University, but there was just no other on-campus housing available. They apologized and put her on a waiting list, but other than that, said there was nothing else that could be done.

The only people she knew in town were Tessa, who'd be leaving soon, and Miranda—and by extension, Miranda's crazy friends. She'd pulled out her phone countless times, wanting to text her cousin—or hoping Miranda would text her, but neither had happened. She didn't know if Miranda may have felt guilty for freaking her out—scaring her half to death, honestly—or maybe she wanted to give Maia some much needed space. In any case, Maia wouldn't be the one to break radio silence.

She made it through her last final and headed up the stairs to Professor Kennedy's office with a sigh. She was tired. Sleep eluded her lately, marred by strange dreams she couldn't remember when she awoke. Muffling a yawn, she knocked lightly on the professor's door frame, drawing his attention from a paper he was marking up with swift strokes of a ball point pen. Professor Joseph Kennedy was the fulfillment of every stereotype of the typical professor, from the graying temples and horn-rimmed glasses, to the suede elbow patches on the tweed blazer hanging off the back of his chair.

"Ms. Sheridan, this is a surprise," he said, straightening the stack of papers and setting it aside. "I'd assumed all the students had already fled for the holidays."

She smiled, despite the panic his words set aflutter in her stomach. "Soon. I was just hoping to catch you before you left. Do you have a moment?"

He motioned to the seat in front of the desk. "Of course. What can I do for you?"

Maia slid into the chair and dug in her backpack for her copy of The Order journal. "I was hoping you could help me with some translation," she said, sliding the papers across the desk. "Or maybe direct me to someone who can? I don't really recognize some of the dialects in this document and I'd like to . . ." She paused when she realized he was eyeing the journal with something akin to surprise, his face several shades paler than the moment before, his posture rigid and tense. "Professor?" she prodded. "Is everything all right?"

He started, shaking his head slightly. "Of course," he said, clearing his throat when it came out as a bit of a croak. He reached out tentatively and slid the stack of papers toward him, turning the pages slowly. "Where did you find this?"

"Microfiche," she said, suddenly unsure of what she should say. "It seems to be a journal of some kind. I was thinking I might use it for my final paper. From what I've been able to make out, it seems like a pretty interesting resource."

"Interesting," he murmured. "Yes, that it is."

She leaned forward a little bit, curiosity winning out over caution. "Can you tell me anything about it? Where it came from?"

He ran a finger over a line of text, silent for a moment.

"What led you to this document?" he asked quietly, his eyes lifting to scrutinize her carefully.

An odd choice of words, she thought, as an unexpected chill ran down her spine. "Led me to it?"

He simply waited, watching her, and for a moment she considered telling him about the whole thing—about her cousin asking her about a symbol on an old chest, about the bizarre story her friends told her . . .

about super powers and quests and fights to save the world.

Ridiculous.

She could almost convince herself of that.

Maia swallowed and looked down at the journal, unable to meet his eyes for some reason. "Nothing *led* me to it," she said with a shrug. "I was looking through some old microfiche, trying to figure out a subject for my final. You said we needed to focus on a person or group of people that had a significant influence on society through at least three generations." She was babbling now, unable to stop. "And I came across the journal and got curious about this Order and who they were and what they did, and why this journal seemed to have been handed down for centuries. It seemed like it might be a good resource for my paper."

She looked up at him finally, forcing a smile. "If I can figure out what it says."

His eyes narrowed slightly and she had the strangest feeling that he didn't believe her. That he knew there was more to it than that. But instead of calling her on it, he nodded slowly.

"I actually am familiar with this," he said, running a finger idly across the paper. "I'd be happy to help you with your research." He tapped the paper once then flipped the stack closed and handed it to her before opening a drawer and withdrawing a business card. He turned it over and scribbled on the back.

"I will be checking my university email periodically over the break," he said, "but it will be easier to reach me with my personal account. I'm giving you my cell number as well, but it will probably be easier to communicate via email. The cell service can be pretty spotty around my house."

Maia reached for the card he held out to her. "I assumed you lived in town."

He stood to put some files into a satchel. "About twenty miles north. We have a little place—a gentlemen's farm, I suppose you'd call it. My wife prefers country living."

"Sounds nice." Miranda tucked the card into her pocket.

He slipped on his jacket. "I'm afraid I have to leave," he said. "But call or email me when you're ready and we can figure out a time to meet."

"Really? Over break?" she asked, surprised.

Professor Kennedy slung his satchel over his shoulder and crossed the room to open the door for her. "We have a lot to cover," he replied. "And in this case, I'd say time is of the essence." He stared at her, unblinking for a moment, as if he were trying to send her a silent message.

Maia broke eye contact, the nerves and panic

rearing their ugly heads once again. "Thank you," she muttered as she left his office and all but ran down the stairs. Her instinct told her Professor Kennedy knew more—a lot more—than she had thought he might. And she wasn't all that sure she wanted to hear what he had to say.

NINE

The darkness seemed thick, somehow, reaching out and sliding over her skin. She couldn't see through it, and reached up to sweep a hand in front of her, almost expecting the gloom to swirl away before her eyes. It didn't, instead it clung to her, an almost physical presence.

Maia trudged forward, unable to see the mud beneath her feet, although she could hear and feel the squelching beneath her. She didn't know where she was going, only that she had to keep walking.

An unfamiliar voice shouted behind her and Maia whirled, jarred by the sudden change in her surroundings. She now stood in the middle of a clearing, surrounded by trees, with people stumbling and screaming around her.

Fighting. They were fighting.

"Run, Maia!"

Chloe tugged on her arm, dragging her forward as

she watched something over Maia's shoulder with wide, frantic eyes.

Maia looked back to find a column of smoke whirling like a tornado behind them. It reached to the sky, fingers of blackness twisting out and streaming through lightning-laced clouds.

"What is that? Is there a fire?" she asked.

Chloe yanked her behind a tree. "You've got to do it," she said. "Do it now, Maia!"

"Do what? I don't know what's going on."

"We're running out of time!" Chloe grabbed her shoulders, shaking them.

Maia pulled away. "I don't know what you want from me!" She turned to run, only to find the smoke pillar right behind her. She spun back around, but Chloe was nowhere to be found— there was only a barren landscape filled with smoke and flying debris.

"Help!" she shouted, her voice barely audible above the now raging wind. Bits of debris and dirt swirled around her, stinging her cheeks as her hair twisted and tangled across her eyes. She stumbled forward, unsure of where she was going, one step at a time.

There. She could see . . . something—a house, barely visible through the storm. She staggered forward, arm held up to shield her eyes as much as possible. The house loomed in the distance, blue with a peaked roof and white front porch—a refuge from the storm raging around her. She tripped over something in her path and fell to a knee, pain shooting up her leg and across her palm as she scraped it on a rock.

Or was it a rock?

Maia blinked and the storm was gone. No trees. No dirt or smoke. Just a quiet night on an unfamiliar street. She knelt on a sidewalk, apparently after tripping on the curb, her palm stinging, but not bleeding from catching her fall on the cement

"What the—"

She got to her feet, a chill seeping through her, and she realized she was barefoot, dressed only in the t-shirt and flannel pants she'd worn to bed—

Bed. A dream. Good lord, she'd been sleepwalking.

Rubbing her bare arms, she turned in a slow circle to try and figure out exactly where she was. It was an ordinary street in an ordinary neighborhood. In the distance to her right, she could hear multiple sirens, but where she was, everything was quiet, the street-lights casting a golden glow on the sidewalk. She shivered, still unsettled by her dream, and considered her next course of action. Maybe she could knock and ask to use a phone. It was the middle of the night, but maybe someone would take pity on a half-dressed, freaked out sleepwalker. She turned to focus on the house before her and froze.

A blue house with a peaked roof and a white front porch.

The house from her dream.

She stumbled back off the curb and bumped into a car. A police car, she realized when she turned around, still in shock.

Perfect.

The officer rolled down the window. "You all right, miss?"

"Umm . . ." She swept her hair back from her face, trying to calm her racing heart, and determinedly *not* looking back at the house. "I guess I've been sleepwalking," she admitted, flexing her toes on the cold asphalt. "I don't suppose you could give me a ride back to campus?"

"Sure," he said. "Get in."

She sat huddled in the back of the squad car, only half-listening to the cop talking about some incident in town. Maia had never sleepwalked before. Never had trouble sleeping or even had such a vivid dream, to be honest. She couldn't understand what was wrong with her.

"—out by yourself at night. It's not safe." The cop caught her eye in the rearview mirror and she scrambled to try and make sense of what he was saying.

"I'm sorry?"

He shook his head as if to mourn the existence of young people in an otherwise sane world.

"I said, with all the trouble in town lately, it's really not safe for you to be out alone at night."

Instead of arguing that she was perfectly capable of taking care of herself—which she had to admit might be hard to prove, given that she was walking around in her pajamas—her curiosity won out.

"What kind of trouble?" she asked.

"You haven't heard?"

"Guess I've been a little busy, you know, with finals and everything."

"And you haven't heard about the problems we've been having?" He shook his head again, muttering almost to himself. "Media's falling down on the job again." He glanced back at her. "It's been a weird couple months. It started out with stupid stuff—fist fights, minor property damage, more domestic disturbances than usual. But it's been escalating lately. We've had a few near riots this week and nobody can figure out why."

"Is it gangs?"

He laughed. "In Gatesburg? No . . . nothing like that. That's what's so weird. The people getting in trouble are just normal people. PTA moms and businessmen and teenagers who we've never had problems with before. I don't get it." He rubbed his jaw, thinking to himself, before he stopped at a red light.

"Anyway, nothing you need to worry about. We have everything under control." He turned around, his arm across the back of the seat and his wristwatch clicked against the grate separating the front of the car from the back.

"I just want you to understand that you shouldn't be out at night. At least not until everything gets back to normal around here. Gatesburg is usually a nice, quiet town."

"That's what they always say in the movies before everything goes to pieces," Maia said dryly.

The cop laughed. "Yeah, well, luckily it's not that exciting around here. I'm sure this will all blow over soon."

Maia directed him to her dorm, and he stopped at the rear entrance and rounded the car to open the back door for her.

"Well, thank you for the ride," Maia said as she got out.

"No problem," he replied with a salute. "You have a good night."

"Thank you." Maia hurried up the walk, and he watched to make sure she unlocked the front door before he drove away. She entered quietly, but the dorm was silent, and she tiptoed back to her room and dove under the covers, wrapping herself in the blankets as she tried to warm up. Whether it was the cold temperature outside, the disturbing nightmare, or the odd feeling she got as the police officer told her what was happening in Gatesburg, she wasn't sure.

It took a long time for her to fall back to sleep.

The next afternoon, Maia sat dejectedly on her bed, hugging her knees to her chest and staring unseeingly at Tessa's old bed across the room. The sheets and pillows were gone, only a few stray pieces of blue sticky tack on the wall marked the places where her numerous posters and photos had decorated the plain white walls. She'd left two hours ago to catch her flight and Maia had spent the time since scanning the Internet for a place to live, to no avail.

Her grumbling stomach and lack of anything edible in the mini-fridge finally forced her to put on shoes and head down to the dining hall for something to eat. The lines were short for the last meal before Christmas break, but she paused briefly to scan the bulletin board hanging by the door, hoping the perfect housing option would miraculously appear pinned to the corkboard.

Nothing.

She let out a huge, self-indulgent sigh and the papers fluttered a little in front of her. Maia was about to turn on her heel and head in for some food, but the corner of a flyer caught her eye. It had been hidden by another poster but she could just see the corner of a phone number peeking out. She moved the poster aside and found a flyer for a room for rent near campus. All of the phone number slips had been ripped off except one, which gave her pause. Most likely, it was an old flyer and all of the rooms were already rented. Still, she ripped off the last number with a tiny surge of hope, and took out her phone to call.

Then she froze, a chill running down her spine. With trembling fingers, she lifted the poster covering the flyer and pushed it aside, revealing the picture of the house with the room for rent.

A blue house with a peaked roof.

"No," she whispered, ripping the flyer off the bulletin board, unable to believe what she was seeing.

But it was real. It was the house she'd dreamed of. The same house she'd sleepwalked to in the middle of the night.

She stood staring at the image printed on the paper, wishing she'd never seen it. Something strange—very strange—was going on. And Maia was quickly realizing that there was no escaping it.

She clenched her fist, crumpling the flyer in her hand, and walked out of the dining hall, her appetite gone. Wandering around campus in a daze, she eventually found herself in front of the library and sat on a bench out front, tugging her coat even tighter around her.

After a while, she took a deep breath and put the flyer on her lap, smoothing the creases out so she could see the house more clearly. There was no doubt in her mind that it was the same house. But what did it mean?

She swallowed, took out her phone, and dialed.

"And the kitchen's through here," the landlord said, leading her through the house. Once Maia had made the decision to call, she pressed to view the house that same evening. When the landlord had given her the address, any doubts she'd had that the house was the one she'd sleepwalked to had vanished, not that there were many to begin with.

Remarkably, when she stood in front of the blue Victorian, instead of fear and anxiety, she'd felt only a sense of resolution—of inevitability. It was as if everything had been leading to that moment, and she only had to accept it.

Not that she had much choice, with the proof

standing in front of her, all two stories and leaded glass windows and peaked roof of it.

Of course, the fact the house was cute was a bonus, and as soon as the landlord started the tour, Maia knew she wanted to live there. She could see evidence of the house's other occupants—an open textbook on the dining room table, a couple bowls drying in a rack next to the sink—but her potential roommates seemed to be out at the moment.

The landlord led her upstairs. "Two rooms are occupied, but you have your choice of the two down there—" he pointed over the handrail to the hall off the kitchen—"or this one." He swung open a door and Maia's breath caught as soon as she walked through it. It wasn't anything special, not really. Just a small room with a single bed, a matching dresser, a small desk, and a tiny closet. But the view through the octagonal window over the bed drew her to it immediately. In the distance, the peak of Mt. Butler gleamed white against the blue sky, and she knew this room was hers.

"I'll take it," she murmured.

"Great!" the landlord—Mr. James—said. "Come on downstairs and we'll take care of the paperwork. When would you like to move in?"

Maia turned to him with a sheepish smile. "Now?" she asked. "I have all of my stuff in my car. You were kind of my last hope."

Mr. James nodded. "Well, lucky we found each other then," he said before leading her back down to the kitchen.

They sat at the table and Maia signed a lease, then wrote a check for the deposit. She thanked the landlord and was just about to follow him out to unload her car when the front door swung open, and two familiar faces appeared.

"Maia?" Miranda blinked at her in surprise. "What are you doing here?"

"Oh, you two know each other," Mr. James said. "That's a happy coincidence. Maia here is your new roommate."

"Roommate?" Chloe said. "You're living here?"

"Didn't see that one coming?" Miranda asked wryly.

"Nope."

"Well, it looks like you have the help you need to unload," Mr. James said to Maia. "So if there's nothing else, I should be going."

Maia opened her mouth to tell him to stop. Tell him she'd changed her mind. But just as quickly, she slammed it shut. She had no choice. This was her home now. And apparently, she shared it with Chloe and Miranda. She couldn't even find it in herself to be surprised. All roads led to this moment. And she, apparently, was just along for the ride.

"Thank you," she told Mr. James quietly.

He nodded at the three of them and walked out the front door, closing it quietly behind him.

She stood, staring after him for a long moment, trying to compose herself. It was fine. It was no big deal. She'd just ignore it. Pretend that craziness hadn't even happened. She'd avoid Miranda as much as she could —*definitely* avoid Chloe and her other weird friends— and work on her paper. She'd spend most of her time in the library, anyway. And Professor Kennedy had offered his own personal library to aid in her research, as well. She'd hardly even be around, she'd be so busy.

So, yeah. It would be fine.

Maia took a deep breath and turned to face Chloe and Miranda. "I've got to get my stuff," she said.

"We can help," they replied simultaneously.

"No . . . no, that's fine," Maia said, suddenly frantic to get out of the house and get some fresh air. "It's not much, so . . ." They both looked so uncomfortable that Maia felt she had to say something.

"Can you let me get settled?" she asked. "Then . . . then maybe we can talk?" She walked out the front door before they could say anything more and made her way to her car, parked along the curb in front of the house. When she came back inside, carrying a box of sheets and towels, Chloe and Miranda were gone. Their bedroom doors were closed, and as she passed one of them, she could make out low voices inside.

Relieved at the temporary reprieve, she unloaded her car in a few more trips, then started to unpack. She had just finished making her bed when there was a quiet knock at the door. With a deep, calming breath, she walked over and opened the door.

Miranda stood in the hall, nervously chewing on her lip for a moment. Then she shook her head with a huff and threw herself at Maia, hugging her tightly.

"I'm so sorry," she said. "We shouldn't have overwhelmed you like that."

Maia let out a soft breath and hugged Miranda back.

"It's okay."

"No, it's not," her cousin said, squeezing her once more before letting her go. "You were clearly uncomfortable and we kept pushing—"

"It's fine." Maia shook her head, not wanting to think about that day again. About the way that girl had just . . . vanished.

How . . .

She shut down that train of thought right away. Denial was a powerful thing, and sometimes it was what kept you sane.

"It's really not fine," Miranda said as she followed Maia into the room. "But we don't have to talk about it if you don't want to."

"Thanks," she said quietly.

"And I told the others to stay away until you're ready—I mean, no pressure or anything. Whenever you want to talk about it, that's when we'll talk about it—"

"Miranda—"

"—and nobody will bring it up until—"

"Miranda." Maia smirked as her cousin stopped, mouth half-open. "I thought we weren't going to talk about it."

Miranda blushed and nodded, saying nothing more as she flopped onto the bed. They chattered about other things while Maia put her clothes in the drawers and set up her laptop and school supplies on the small desk in the corner. The room was already feeling like home. She'd set up a few framed photos on top of the dresser, smiling at the mountain as she passed the window, now barely visible in the fading light.

"You should let me do your hair since you're here," Miranda said with a sly grin.

Maia eyed the purple and teal streaks through Miranda's own short hair. "I don't think so."

"Oh come on! You'd look so cute with some blonde streaks—or yellow!"

Maia laughed. "Miranda, I've gone through my

whole life with a bright orange rat's nest. The last thing I need is to draw *more* attention to my hair."

"Oh, shut up. Your hair is gorgeous."

Maia shook her head. She'd come to an uneasy truce with her curls over the years, given up on fighting them and just letting them do their thing. Miranda could pull off the wild colors. Maia . . . not so much.

"Thanks," she said. "But I'm not dyeing it."

Miranda let out a huff. "You're no fun. Chloe won't let me do hers, either."

At the mention of Chloe, the uneasy tension seeped back into the room. They both tried to ignore it, though.

"So," Miranda said, getting off the bed to approach the desk and eye the stacks of books and papers. "You have a lot of homework over Christmas break?"

"Some," she replied. "You?"

Miranda shrugged. "Just some reading. Nothing too heavy." She caught sight of familiar photocopied pages. "You working on your paper?"

Maia stiffened. "Yes."

Miranda's gaze flashed up to meet hers. "About The Order?"

Maia nodded. "My prof's been great. He offered to help me with the translation over break. I'm going to call him tomorrow about using his research library."

"Really?" Miranda's excitement was palpable. She

was practically vibrating with it. She opened her mouth but snapped it shut. Maia could tell that she was trying not to pressure her, that she was dying to ask her more about the journal, but didn't want to break her word that they weren't going to discuss it.

Maia felt bad. Miranda was her cousin, her closest family member other than her own mother. And regardless of what had happened, whatever she was involved in with her weird friends, Maia wasn't going to cut her off.

"You could—" She leaned against the desk and reached over to flip idly through some pages. "I mean, when I go over to meet with him about the book . . . You could come, if you want."

"Really?" Miranda grinned, bouncing on her toes.

"Just you," Maia said quickly. "Not everybody."

"Yeah, sure, of course," she replied, nodding. "Just me. I'll go along and I promise, I'll just listen. I won't ask him a bunch of questions."

Maia rolled her eyes. "You can ask him questions." She hesitated, unsure of how to phrase her next comment. "Just don't, you know, bring up the whole . . ." She lifted her hands and wiggled her fingers around her head in the universal symbol for crazy weirdness. "You know?"

"Right, yeah, of course." Miranda flushed slightly. "Mum's the word."

Focused intently on the papers as she bent a corner, then flattened it out, Maia cleared her throat. "I don't really understand what's going on, or how you're involved, or *why* you're trying to drag me into all of this—"

"Maia—"

"—but." She lifted her gaze to meet her cousin's. "*But* you're my family and I don't want to lose that."

"You won't."

"And if you need me, I mean, to talk to about . . . whatever." Maia waved a hand again. "I want you to know I'm here."

Miranda toyed with her earring, her eyes narrowing. "Last time you ran away."

Maia's hackles rose. "Can you blame me? You guys—"

"No, no . . . I don't blame you, I told you I don't." She walked back over to sit on the bed, the comforter billowing up around her. "But . . . I want you to know it wasn't a trick or a game or anything like that. It was—it *is* real."

Maia opened her mouth to reply, but Miranda barreled on. "And I know you're not ready to deal with it all, but you'll have to someday . . . someday *soon*. One way or the other. But I want you to know I'm here for you, too, Maia. So just . . . you know, know that."

There were a lot of things Maia could have said to

that. She knew she couldn't go on ignoring what they'd told her—what she'd *seen*—the inexplicable, impossible things she'd seen in that research room. But she had never been one to act on impulse. Maia was a thinker, an analyzer, and she needed to absorb what she'd been told—research, contemplate, and consider—before she could do anything else.

So instead of pouring out platitudes or reassurances to her cousin, she simply said, "Thanks," and finished her unpacking.

TEN

"You're awfully quiet. Everything okay?" Miranda asked as they drove out of town toward Professor Kennedy's house. Maia had hesitated to email him at first, unsure if he really wanted her to disrupt his holiday. But once she did, he'd responded almost immediately and invited them both over.

She hadn't told her cousin about her late night sleepwalking session, or the strange dream about their house . . . the latest in a long list of strange things in her life recently. Things she still refused to contemplate too deeply.

Denial was a wonderful thing.

"I'm fine," she replied, stifling a yawn. "Just didn't sleep too well last night."

Miranda shot her a sharp look. "Bad dreams?"

Maia shrugged and avoided meeting her eyes. "Can't remember."

Miranda hummed as if she wasn't quite sure she

believed her, but turned back to look at the road. Pavement turned to gravel as they wound their way out of town and down a long driveway to a two-story farmhouse. Frost covered the wilted flowers in the front yard, but the brick walkway had been recently swept. They parked in front of the detached garage and exchanged a glance before approaching the front door.

"It's kind of weird, isn't it," Miranda asked as they approached the front door, "for your professor to invite you to his house?"

"The house he shares with his wife and son," she replied. "It's not *that* weird. He's just trying to help me out."

"Okay, if you say so. I have pepper spray in my purse, just in case."

Maia rolled her eyes. "I'm pretty sure we won't need that." She raised her hand to knock, but paused to hiss at her cousin. "Now, behave!"

Miranda held up her hands in surrender and Maia narrowed her eyes with one more finger point before turning to knock on the door.

The door swung open to reveal a woman holding a pile of curly brown hair atop her head. She was barefoot and wore faded, holey jeans and a long sleeved tie-dyed t-shirt, knotted at her trim waist and spattered with paint. Her glasses were slightly askew over warm brown eyes and she shoved them up her nose before viciously snapping an elastic band around her hair, taming it only slightly.

"You must be . . . Maia?" she said, looking back and forth between them.

"That's me," she replied. "This is my cousin Miranda. She has . . . um . . . interests in my research as well."

The woman rolled her eyes and blew an errant strand of hair out of her face. "Research, research, research. That's all we hear around here. You'd think certain people actually forget they're on vacation!" She all but shouted the last few words back into the house and Maia could barely make out a muffled reply.

"If this is a bad time . . ." she said.

"What?" The woman looked genuinely stunned for a moment, then smiled sheepishly. "Oh, no . . . no, of course not. Come on in." She closed the door behind them and led them down the hall. "I'm just giving my husband a hard time. The guy works all the time, but that's who he is. We haven't been married for almost twenty-five years because I ever tried to change him. I'm Daisy, by the way."

"I'm sorry, but you seem really familiar," Miranda said. "Do you know—"

Pounding footsteps down the stairs drew their attention.

"Mom, I've asked you before to quit leaving boxes

of condoms in my . . . bath . . . room . . ." A tall, lean guy with spiky brown hair and glasses came to an abrupt stop when he spotted them, his cheeks flaming and the aforementioned box held high above his head.

"I, uh, didn't know anyone was here." He seemed to notice the box and jerked his hand behind his back.

Daisy approached him and patted his cheek. "Sweetie, how many times do I have to tell you sex is nothing to be ashamed of? And the old ones were expired."

"Mom!" The guy looked ready to melt into the floor in embarrassment. Maia couldn't blame him, but wasn't sure what she could do to relieve it.

Miranda cleared her throat and raised a hand in a finger wiggling wave. "Um, hey, Dylan." Her own cheeks were pink and Maia wondered if it was more than secondhand embarrassment for the boy.

His mouth dropped open. "Miranda! What are—" He fumbled, dropped the condoms, and kicked the box under the hall table. "What are you doing here?"

"Well, I guess we're here to see your . . . dad?"

"Oh, oh right. Yeah." He nodded vigorously. "Yeah, he mentioned a student was coming over. I guess that'd be you, right?" He finger-gunned at Maia. "Of course it is. Right. I'm just going to go—" He hooked a thumb over his shoulder. "Go and die of embarrassment, okay? Great. Yeah, good talk."

He fled up the stairs and Miranda, almost in a daze, watched him go. When she saw Maia staring at her, she shrugged, cheeks flaming. "He works at the coffee shop."

"Oh yeah," Maia said, finally connecting the dots. "I thought he looked familiar." They followed Daisy down the hall and Maia leaned in to whisper, "You guys a thing?"

"What? No!" Miranda's cheeks flamed again as she glanced at Daisy, obviously hoping she hadn't heard.

Maia's lips quirked. "He's kind of cute."

"Shut up," Miranda hissed.

Maia held back a giggle as Daisy escorted them toward what she assumed was Professor Kennedy's library at the back of the house. She'd have to explore the whole Dylan situation later.

"Honey? Your students are here," Daisy said, knocking once on the door before swinging it open.

The professor was seated behind a large wooden desk, bookshelves lining the wall behind and to the left a large window dominated the wall to the right. He stood and dropped his glasses on the desk.

"Maia, come on in," he said.

"This is my cousin, Miranda."

"Miranda." He smiled at her and held out a hand. "Nice to meet you."

"You, too. I hope you don't mind me tagging along."

"Not at all," he replied, smiling over her shoulder at his wife, who pulled the door closed behind her. "Always room in my library for a fellow historian."

"Well, I'm not sure I qualify," she said, "but thank you."

He motioned to the low leather chairs before his desk. "Have a seat. I actually was working on your translation."

The two girls pulled out their laptops as Professor Kennedy sat down behind his desk and reached for his copy of the book about The Order.

"The initial entries are in Latin, some old Saxon, possibly dating around the 9th century," he said. "But they point to the so called Order being in existence long before that."

"How long?" Miranda asked.

"Centuries. Millennia possibly," the professor replied with a shrug. "It's not definitive."

"So what exactly is The Order?" Maia asked.

He leaned back in his chair, rocking slowly. "Basically, The Order is a group of individuals who come together to defend humanity against the forces of evil and chaos."

Maia frowned. "So, it's some kind of club? Or a fraternal organization? Like the Masons or something?"

"No, not exactly." He studied her for a moment

over tented fingers, but just as she was about to look away, he took a deep breath.

"The members of The Order are carefully chosen each generation, according to the needs of the time. Each is given a certain gift to aid in their quest—either to protect or to fight."

Maia's stomach flipped wildly. "What kind of gift?"

His intense gaze didn't falter. "It depends on what is needed. There are references to strength, speed . . . the ability to manipulate time, invisibility, illusion, foreseeing the future—"

"But that's impossible," Miranda said, eyes narrowing.

His lips twitched. "Of course it is."

Maia cleared her throat. "So, the book is a record of this Order, through the generations?"

The professor nodded and leaned forward on his desk. "Yes. According to the journal, not all gifts are bestowed in every generation—some have been more than others, again, depending on what is needed. But there are two who are always present—the Seer and the Scribe. The Seer is to watch for what's coming-"

"And the Scribe is to keep the record," Miranda said quietly.

"Exactly," he replied. "If there's a need, the Seer will know, and the others will be summoned."

Maia opened her mouth, but no words came out. Nerves vibrated through her body and she was quickly coming to realize that there was no room for denial anymore.

Nowhere to run.

She cleared her throat. "Summoned by whom?"

"It's not clear," he said. "The closest thing to an explanation is in one of the early entries. Here, let me see if I can find it." He flipped through the pages and stopped, running a finger along a line of text.

"Before time, before all that is, there was chaos. But chaos was tamed and all that is came into being. Still, it remains, chained in the depths, awaiting its opportunity to return, to regain its power. It feeds on discord and strife, and when it grows strong enough, it emerges to wreak havoc and destruction on all creation. The balance must be reclaimed, and so the forces of order are called forth."

Miranda tapped at her keyboard. "Order and chaos," she mumbled.

"Yes," Professor Kennedy said. "Good and evil. Yin and Yang. Whatever you want to call it, according to this, the balance, or whatever is in charge of keeping the balance, calls The Order together when it is needed."

His words hung in the air, an uneasy tension pulsing around them. Maia could almost feel eyes on her—the professor's, curious and expectant. Miranda's, nervous and hopeful.

Maia snapped her laptop shut. "Well, this is very interesting," she said, panic making her voice a bit higher than normal. "We don't want to take up any more of your time, Professor."

"Maia—"

"I mean, the mythology is quite intriguing. Duality is a common theme in many belief systems worldwide, and this text definitely casts a new light on it, but I don't know. Perhaps it's a bit too complex for my paper." She stood up abruptly and crammed her laptop into her bag. "Miranda, we should go."

To her credit, her cousin didn't argue, but packed up her things as well.

"Maia," Professor Kennedy said sharply. "Hold on a moment."

"I really don't think—"

"Why don't you tell me why you're really here," he said, looking at her, then at Miranda. "What do you *really* want to ask me?"

Maia snatched up her bag and grabbed Miranda's arm before she could say a word.

"Nothing," she said. "I don't want to ask you anything. I think I'll find another topic for my paper. Thank you for your time, Professor."

His jaw tensed and he gave her a tight nod. "You know where to find me if you change your mind."

Maia practically dragged Miranda from the house, stumbling a little in the driveway. She threw her bag into the back seat and slammed her door, her heart racing.

"What's wrong with you?" Miranda asked as she started the car. "How long are you going to ignore this?"

"I'm not ignoring anything," she snapped.

"Maia—"

"Can you just drive? Please?" she asked, closing her eyes and taking a steadying breath. "I know we have to talk about this. I know I—I *know* okay? But can we get out of here first?"

Miranda sighed and turned around quickly, spewing dirt as they sped down the driveway. She didn't speak, but Maia could feel her glancing at her every few seconds.

"What do I have to do?" she asked finally, watching the passing scenery. "I mean, if I decide to buy into all of this . . ." She waved a hand to indicate the insanity of it all. "What do I have to do?"

"You don't *have* to do anything," Miranda replied quietly. "But if Professor Kennedy is right, we need you. We need you for what's coming. Whether you join us or not is your decision."

"And if I do? Decide to join you?" The words almost stuck in her throat.

Miranda tapped the steering wheel with a finger. "You open the chest in Chloe's attic. There will be something in there that will give you a gift of some kind."

"Like freezing time?"

"Well, that one's already spoken for," Miranda said, her lips quirking slightly. "But yeah, something like that, maybe. We don't really know."

She turned to look at her cousin. "And what about you? Do you have a gift?"

"Me? Nah." Miranda shrugged. "I don't see anything in the chest, but after talking to the professor . . ." She chewed on her lip.

"What?"

"I think, maybe . . . maybe I'm the Scribe? I'm supposed to keep a record or whatever, for future generations? I don't know. I've kind of been doing that already, you know? Maybe that's why."

Maia nodded slowly. "You realize this is crazy, right?"

She laughed. "Oh, yeah. Definitely." She turned to look at her. "But it's real, Maia. It's totally real. I swear."

Maia turned to look back out the window, her mind whirling with thoughts, but her heart already knowing what she had to do.

"Let's go home."

When they pulled to a stop at the curb in front of the house, Maia sat and stared at it for a long moment.

"What is it?" Miranda asked.

Maia sighed. "I saw this in a dream," she said. "A rather frightening one, to be honest. When I woke up, I found myself standing right here in the street. I walked here in my sleep."

Miranda's brows shot up. "That ever happen before?"

"No."

"Interesting."

"Yeah." She huffed out a laugh. "I guess there's no denying that I'm in this, whatever *this* is. Everywhere I turn, there's something else drawing me in. The journal. The dream. The sleepwalking. This house—" Maia gestured toward it. "I can't really run away from it anymore."

Miranda reached out and squeezed her hand. "No, I guess not. I mean, you have a choice. But it looks like you have to make it."

"No ignoring it."

"Nope." Miranda shot her a sympathetic smile before getting out of the car.

Maia followed her up the steps and into the house, unsurprised to find Chloe waiting for them at the bottom of the stairs. She turned to lead them to the second floor, and up a pull-down ladder at the end of the hall. They emerged in the attic, and Maia's eyes immediately settled on the chest in the corner.

It looked pretty ordinary, actually. Maia wasn't sure exactly what she'd expected—maybe some ancient runes or sparkling fairy dust—but other than the spiral engraving on top, it looked like something you'd find in anyone's attic.

"Now what?" she asked.

Chloe and Miranda stood behind her, flanking her as if for moral support. The air in the attic was slightly stale and musty, dust motes floating in the glow from the window.

"Just open it up," Chloe said. "And tell us what you see."

"Don't you know?" Maia asked her with a sharp look. "I thought you could see the future."

Chloe smiled softly. "I see possible futures, sometimes. But not everything and not always in detail."

"Sounds frustrating."

"You have no idea."

Maia inhaled slowly and let it out just as slowly, then straightened her shoulders and approached the chest. Done with delays and indecision, she wasted no more time and lifted the lid. Inside, she spotted a mass of red fabric wadded up in a corner.

"What is it?" Miranda asked.

"I'm not sure. Some kind of cloth." She glanced at her. "So I just pick it up?"

Miranda shrugged, and she took that as a yes.

Maia reached in and grabbed the fabric, surprised that it seemed almost warm, the threads silky between her fingers. She held it up and gave it a shake.

"It's . . . I think it's a cape." She looked at Chloe and Miranda, who were watching her wide-eyed. "You really don't see it?"

They shook their heads.

"What do I do now?" Maia asked.

Chloe frowned. "The others only had to touch it. Maybe . . . put it on?"

Maia nodded and swept the cape up around and over her shoulders. The instant the fabric settled, a bright light filled the space, as warmth and a kind of electric hum pulsed through her body. Then the light dimmed and the cape just . . . vanished, the light shimmering along her skin before it too disappeared.

"What happened?" Maia turned around in confusion, but when she looked up at Chloe and Miranda, their mouths were open, their expressions stunned.

"What?" Maia asked.

"How do you feel?" Miranda asked. She took a step

166

toward her, and reached out, somewhere to Maia's left. "Can you hear me?"

"Of course I can hear you. What's the matter?"

Miranda looked back at Chloe, who laughed. "You're invisible."

"I'm . . . what are you talking about?" She held up a hand, wiggling her fingers. "I'm not invisible."

"Here. Come over here." Chloe crossed the room and ripped off a dusty sheet covering an old dresser and mirror. "See for yourself."

Maia's heart thudded heavy in her chest as she approached the mirror. But when she looked into it, she could see Chloe . . . Miranda, behind her, but no . . . Maia.

"Whoa." She touched her face and it was there. She could feel it. But she couldn't see it. "This is completely freaky."

She stared at the mirror and slowly she faded into view, transparent and colorless, but growing more solid with every breath. Maia stared, wide-eyed at her reflection and poked at her cheek, unsettled. "Do you see me now?" she asked Chloe.

"Yeah, you're back," she said with a smile. "Pretty cool power. Now you just have to learn to control it."

"But don't worry," Miranda said, throwing an arm over her shoulders. "We have a lot of experience with that now."

ELEVEN

The sun was setting by the time Miranda could get out of the house without Maia asking any questions. Her cousin had been working on accessing her power all day with Chloe—and Wren, who'd come by as soon as she'd heard that Maia had opened the chest—and was exhausted, lying half-asleep on the couch watching some mindless television. Miranda had muttered something about wanting ice cream and Maia had waved her off without asking any questions.

Which was good. Miranda had always been a terrible liar.

She drove to the edge of town, retracing her path from earlier. A police car and two fire trucks raced by going the opposite direction, toward town, and she pulled off to the side to let them pass before continuing on her way. She wound down the long driveway and paused in her stopped car, breathing deeply.

What was she doing? Maybe she was losing it—seeing things that weren't really there. It wouldn't be the first time Miranda had exaggerated things in her own mind.

But no, she knew deep inside that this was what she needed to do—where she needed to be. So she got out of the car and made her way to the front door, lifting her fist to knock before she could change her mind.

It didn't surprise her that Professor Kennedy opened the door himself, almost as if he'd been waiting for her.

He nodded slowly. "I thought you might be back. At first I'd assumed it was Maia, but no, this makes more sense." He stood back, waving her inside. "Come on in."

She passed in front of him and headed toward the library, feeling him behind her as she went. She stood right inside the door, shifting from one foot to the other nervously as he walked behind the desk, and moved a stack of books off a shelf to access a safe behind them.

Miranda had a feeling she knew what was in that safe, but she didn't speak, the hush in the room solemn, almost reverent, as if something important were taking place.

A click echoed and Professor Kennedy reached

into the safe and withdrew a stack of papers and set them aside. Then he pulled it out.

The book.

The *original* book.

It was a deep red, darker than it had looked on microfiche, the pages yellowed with age, but undamaged—no cracks or tears in the paper or the leather cover. He turned around and held it out toward her, the embossed spiral on the cover identical to the one on the chest in Chloe's attic.

"I thought perhaps it was Maia," he said again when she stepped forward for a closer look. "But I've been wrong before."

Her gaze flicked up to meet his. "How do you know it's me?"

He shrugged. "*You* know, don't you?"

Instead of replying, she focused back on the journal. "It's thicker than I expected."

"Well, the most recent entries were not transferred to microfiche."

She pursed her lips thoughtfully and picked up the book, flipping through to the last few pages, relieved to find modern English in a clean, block script. "So, you're the Scribe?" she asked.

"No, not me," he said with a quiet laugh. "My brother, Liam. He got the book when he turned sixteen, passed on by the former Scribe—a man from back East somewhere. He never told me the details. Liam passed away two years later. Leukemia."

"I'm sorry."

He dipped his chin in acknowledgement. "He asked me to take the book, said the next Scribe would come to me when the time was right."

She skimmed a few pages, stopping at a familiar name. "Therese?"

"Hmm?"

She pointed to the book. "There's a reference here to someone named Therese."

"Ah, yes." He leaned forward, his elbows on the desk. "The Seer at the time. She's the one who saw you coming."

"Chloe's mother's name was Therese," she said quietly. "I highly suspect that's no coincidence."

His lips quirked. "I would assume so. Chloe has inherited her mother's power, perhaps?"

"I don't know," she replied. "If Chloe's mom had visions, I don't think she knew about it."

"Well, I suppose it could be another Therese."

Miranda laughed. "Oh, I doubt that. After everything we've experienced lately, I would be more surprised if it was someone *other* than Chloe's mom."

He smiled, his eyes on the ceiling as if puzzling out

a mystery. "If so, it's interesting. The connection between the generations. Chloe inheriting her Seer's gift from her mother. You, her best friend, are the Scribe. Maia is your cousin—" He gave her an expectant look.

"She, uh, can be invisible."

"Ah, yes—one of the rarer gifts. And the others?"

"We go to school with Beck. He's got strength and speed. Wren moved into town a few months ago. She can stop time."

He sat up. "That's five."

"Yeah. But according to Chloe's visions, there are a couple more, I think. We haven't met them yet."

Professor Kennedy frowned slightly.

"What? Is that important?" she asked.

"Perhaps," he murmured, half to himself. "It's just that there are only two instances in the journal of an Order that large. And none has been bigger than six members."

"What does that mean?" Miranda's stomach churned, already suspecting the answer.

"Well, from what I understand, it means the threat you're facing is big."

"How big?" Miranda asked.

The professor rubbed a hand over his face. "Bigger than it's been in a very long time. Stronger, too."

"Perfect," Miranda muttered. "How did I know you were going to say that?"

The professor rounded his desk and sat back down. "I can help, you know. I don't have a gift, but I can help."

"How?" She sat down across from him, her fingers trailing absently over the book cover.

"Help you prepare," he said. "Teach you some defense. Guide you as best I can. I'm pretty familiar with the contents of that." He tipped his head toward the book.

Miranda nodded. "I suppose we could use all the help we can get."

He placed his elbows on the desk, tenting his fingers and tapping them on his lips as he thought for a moment. "You and I, we may not have special abilities, but we have a part to play in all of this, you know?"

"You make it sound like a game."

He huffed. "No, it's definitely not a game. But there are rules. And between the two of us, we can help figure those out. Interpret what those who came before us have learned and use it to our advantage."

Miranda flipped through the pages in the book. "So, the answers are all in here?"

"Not all of them, no," he replied. "But it's definitely a place to begin."

She paused for a moment, not meeting his eyes . . . not wanting to ask the question, but knowing she had to. "Can we win?" she whispered.

"We can."

Miranda looked up finally, needing to see the truth in his expression. "*Will* we?"

He met her gaze, fervent and sure. "It's not a matter of *can* or *will*," he said finally. "We *must*. There is no other option. Everything depends on it."

She shook her head with a wry smile. "But no pressure, right?"

Professor Kennedy's lips quirked and he relaxed a bit. "Sorry," he said. "I've been waiting for a long time. I get a little worked up."

"Understandable," she replied as she tucked the book into her bag. "You should join us for training. But, Professor?"

"Yes."

"Tone it down a bit on the *fate of the world depends on us* stuff, okay? At least with the others?" she said. "It's kind of a lot, and we're all still finding our way here."

The professor nodded. "Duly noted."

Her eyes strayed to a pair of worn boxing gloves on his bookshelf. "But if you can teach me to throw a punch, that might be helpful."

His smile widened. "I do believe that can be arranged," he replied.

Gina Talbot stood in the deep shadows outside, down the driveway from the Kennedy house, smacking loudly on a piece of gum as she leaned against a sleek, black car she'd liberated in town. *It* wasn't happy, and it made Gina jumpy . . . uncomfortable.

She liked when It was happy.

"We'll have to step up our timeline," It said, sending a shiver down her spine. "I didn't expect the Scribe to find the journal so quickly."

She spat out her gum and rubbed her aching jaw. "Do you want me to stop her?"

It laughed. "The girl is inconsequential. She's only to keep a record. And this time, the record will show my inevitable victory."

Gina shrugged. It didn't matter to her one way or the other, really.

"The Order is growing," she said quietly. "My son—"

"Your son was an unpleasant surprise," It snapped, irritated. "Stronger than I anticipated. I underestimated him. That won't happen again."

"Will there be more?"

A surge of anger shot through Gina, pain radiating from her core through her limbs—an electric shock hitting every nerve ending. She fell to the ground and curled in on herself, whimpering in pain.

"Don't ask questions you have no business asking," It hissed. "I'll tell you what you need to know, when you need to know it."

The pain eased, but Gina wondered if perhaps *It* didn't know the answer to her question. The anger she'd felt was tinged with something she was pretty sure was frustration.

She didn't dare voice her opinion, however, and forced herself to think of other things as she got to her feet. If she focused, she could hide her thoughts to a degree, and she didn't need It knowing about her doubts.

They didn't matter anyway. Nothing mattered but the end goal. The power. The control.

"Of course," she said instead. "I'll do whatever you ask. You know that."

"Then get back to town," It said. "Time is short and I need to feed."

Gina smiled and got into the car. The cloak and dagger stuff was boring, but the feeding part? That was kind of fun.

She put the car in gear and sped off down the

driveway, heedless of the dust and gravel she sprayed in her wake.

The next morning, the entire group gathered at the Victorian. Maia wasn't entirely sure what it all was about. She'd fallen asleep before Miranda had come home the night before, and in the morning, she'd simply said they were having a group meeting. She'd actually called it an *Assembly of The Order* but Maia wasn't quite to the point where she felt comfortable using archaic titles of mystical unknown origins.

Chloe, ever the gracious host, handed out cups of coffee before settling down on the floor in front of Ethan, who sat in the armchair. Maia, Beck, and Wren took the couch, and Miranda pulled in a chair from the dining table, but didn't bother sitting, instead pacing back and forth, nervous energy almost palpable in the room.

"Are you going to tell us what this is all about?" Maia finally asked her.

Miranda let the drama build for a moment, then, with a flourish, dropped a book onto the center of the table.

Chloe popped up on her knees. "Is that . . ." She

snatched the book, instantly recognizing the cover. "Where did you get this?"

"I went to see Professor Kennedy last night. Turns out, I'm the newest Scribe."

"Wait, what?" Wren asked. "What's a Scribe? What are you talking about?"

Miranda explained about their visit the day before, about the journal and Seers and Scribes and The Order, or what they knew of it now. And how the professor's brother was the previous Scribe.

"And get this," she said, focused on Chloe. "The previous Seer was named Therese."

Chloe's breath caught. "My mom?" Everyone was quiet, watching as she absorbed that information.

"But wait . . ." she said, standing up to lean forward on the table. "Aunt Cara said my mom had . . . *feelings* . . . you know, like me. But she never said anything about a chest or The Order or anything like that."

"Maybe your mom didn't see that it would be an issue," Miranda replied. "Or maybe she would have explained it when you were older and she just . . . didn't get a chance."

Chloe swallowed and nodded, a flash of sadness crossing her features.

Miranda cleared her throat and turned to pace across the room and back. "According to the journal, the number of people in The Order fluctuates in proportion to the upcoming threat. At the time your mom was the Seer, it was only her and Liam, the Scribe. No major threat. Their job was to keep an eye on things, just in case."

"So, if there was no threat, there was no reason to think the rest of The Order would be called in, or whatever," Ethan said.

"Right." Miranda walked back to the table and placed her hands on her hips. "In fact, it's rare for there to be more than two or three members at any given time. Only twice in the history of The Order, from what I've found from reading the journal, has there ever been a group larger than five."

"There are five of us already," Wren pointed out.

"And more on the way," Chloe said. "At least two, that I've seen, although I have no idea who they are or even what they look like. I've only seen them from a distance."

Maia cleared her throat. "And if the size of The Order is proportionate to the size of the threat . . ."

"That's a pretty big threat," Beck said.

Maia threw up her hands. "But we don't even know what it is we're fighting! How in the world do you defeat a pillar of body snatching black smoke?"

"We know more about it than we think," Beck said quietly. "It's been inside me. I know it pretty intimately."

"Right." Miranda jabbed a finger at him and sat back down. "That's an advantage. Beck was able to fight it off. We can use that."

"This is insane," Maia exclaimed. "How are we supposed to fight some ancient evil?"

Miranda counted off on her fingers. "You train. You plan. You work together. And you rely on Chloe's visions to guide you."

Everyone sat back down, silence settling in the room.

"So, where do we train?" Wren asked. "I don't think the back yard here is big enough, and the park's too out in the open."

Ethan hummed. "The school? There's swim practice in the morning, but other than that, nothing much is happening over break. The stadium won't work, but the practice field is surrounded by trees and out of sight from the main roads."

Chloe nodded slowly. "It'd have to be after dark. Maybe eight?"

"Sounds like a plan," said Beck, slapping a hand on the table as he got to his feet. "Now, how about breakfast? We can't save the world on an empty stomach."

Late that night, Chloe made a call.

"Hello?"

"Aunt Cara?"

"Chloe?" Her aunt's voice went from sleepy to alert in one word. "What is it? What's wrong? Are you okay?"

"I'm fine." She glanced at her clock with a wince. "Sorry it's so late."

Aunt Cara muffled a yawn. "Don't be ridiculous. You can call me anytime. How's school?"

"Fine. Good."

"Miranda?"

"She's good," Chloe replied. "We have a new room-mate, too. Maia. She's a grad student."

"Oh, that's nice."

The silence hung on for a moment. "Chloe, what's going on?"

She sighed. "I have to ask you something."

"All right."

"Did my mom—" Chloe tried to organize her thoughts. "Tell me about my mom."

"What . . . what do you want to know?"

"She had—*feelings*—like me."

"Yes," Aunt Cara replied slowly. "Her intuition was unusually strong. Like yours. We've talked about this before."

"I know, but—" Chloe chewed on her lip. "What kinds of things did she do, or know, or whatever?"

"Well, let's see." She could hear a rustling sound, like her aunt was getting comfortable. "Most of it was just little stuff—grabbing an umbrella when there were clear skies because she had a feeling it was going to rain, that kind of thing."

"And she was right?"

Aunt Cara laughed. "Yeah, yeah she usually was."

"Did she—Did she ever have visions?"

The line was quiet, and Chloe could hear her aunt's quiet breaths.

"Aunt Cara?"

"I'm here. Sorry." She sighed. "Therese—She told me you'd ask this someday."

Chloe froze, her stomach swooping. "She did?"

"I can't tell you much," Aunt Cara said. "Therese didn't tell *me* much. She said it was for my own protection, whatever that means. But she did say that one day you'd ask about visions, and she made me memorize what to tell you when you did."

Chloe swallowed, her throat thick. "And what is that?"

"The Order is real," she replied. "You are the Seer. Trust your instincts and rely on your friends. It's the only way to defeat the darkness."

A chill ran over Chloe's skin. "Is that it?"

"That's it," Aunt Cara said, and Chloe could hear the worry in her voice. "Do you know what it means?"

"I think so."

"Chloe, I don't like this. What darkness? What's going on?"

Chloe let out a heavy breath. "I'm not completely sure, just yet. But I'm okay. I promise."

"Maybe I should come out there—"

"You have to trust me," Chloe said, almost desperately. She couldn't do what she needed to do and worry about protecting Aunt Cara at the same time. "I'm okay. I'm safe."

"Are you sure?"

"I'm fine," Chloe said, willing her aunt to believe her. "Mom wouldn't have given you the message if she thought I couldn't handle things, right?"

Aunt Cara hesitated, but finally said, "I suppose. I still don't like it."

Chloe couldn't blame her.

"Promise me, if you need help you'll call," her aunt demanded.

"I promise."

"Chloe—"

"I *promise*." It wasn't really a lie. Her aunt couldn't offer the kind of help Chloe needed anyway. "And I'll see you at Christmas."

"You're bringing Miranda?"

"Of course, and her mom," Chloe replied. "And maybe Maia, too, if she doesn't have other plans."

"The more the merrier." Aunt Cara yawned again. "Love you, girl."

"Love you, too."

She hung up, knowing neither one of them would get much sleep that night, her mother's words repeating over and over again in her mind as she lay there in the dark.

TWELVE

"That's so freaky. Doesn't matter how many times I see it," Miranda said, eyes darting from Maia's invisible hands to the stopwatch in her own. "Five minutes. That's the longest yet."

Maia nodded and relaxed, her hands appearing almost instantly. They'd been at it for over an hour and she'd gone from going totally invisible to practicing with different parts of her body.

"I still don't know what good it is," she said, sitting next to Miranda on her bed. "I mean, what use are invisible hands when fighting a . . . whatever it is we're fighting."

Miranda frowned and leaned back on her hands. "Maybe you should try making something else disappear."

"Something else?"

Miranda shrugged. "Wren brought Beck into her

time-freeze by touching him. Maybe you can do something similar."

Maia stood up and walked slowly around the room before picking up a pen off the desk. "This maybe?"

She nodded. "Probably good to start small."

Maia hefted the pen in her flattened palm, then gripped it tightly, and opened her hand again. "Any idea how I should go about doing this?"

Miranda huffed out a laugh. "Like I should know?" She sat up and clicked the button on the stopwatch a few times as she thought. "You said you could feel your gift, right?"

"Yeah."

"And you can direct it to various parts of your body now, so you know what it feels like to control it."

"Yeah. I guess so."

"So then, you just let it . . . go, maybe?"

"Let it go," Maia said with a doubtful glance at the pen.

"Hey, if you've got a better idea . . ." She tossed the watch on the bed.

Maia sighed. "I don't. Here goes nothing."

"That's the spirit!" Miranda grinned.

Maia shot her a halfhearted glare, then closed her eyes and took a deep breath, focusing on the electric hum deep inside her, like she'd been taught. She could hear Miranda's sharp intake of breath and knew that she'd vanished, but instead of opening her eyes, she did what Miranda had suggested—envisioned the power flowing through her limbs and out her fingertips. Felt it running through her nerve endings, rippling along her skin, and out into the world.

"Maia—"

The pen clutched tightly in her fist, it became almost a part of her. In fact, everything seemed to be part of her—a chain of links from Maia to the pen to the room to the—where did it stop? Instead of growing weaker, the longer she let her gift flow, the stronger it seemed to get. On and on . . . until the ripples became rushing waters and then a surging, raging tide.

"Maia!"

Her eyes flew open and she was met by Miranda's shocked gaze.

"What?" she asked.

"What?" Miranda's mouth opened and closed a couple of times. "*What?* she says. Look!" She pointed to the mirror and it took a moment for Maia to understand what she was seeing.

She was gone. So was the pen. And so was half the room.

Maia could see through the walls to her own bedroom behind her and off to her right, the wall had vanished, revealing the yard and the neighbor's house beyond. The floor was gone in a jagged hole under her feet—empty space through the first floor and at least a yard below that where dirt and rocks formed the edge of her influence.

"Whoa."

"Yeah, whoa," Miranda said with a snort. "Um, can you bring back the room, please?"

Maia hadn't even realized the power was still pulsing through her. She pulled it back, breathing steadily and watching in the mirror as the walls and floor reappeared, then her body shimmered into existence, the pen still gripped in her hand.

"Well, that was interesting," Maia said.

"Interesting, shminteresting," Miranda said, getting up from the bed. "Take my hand and make *me* disappear."

Maia pulled back. "What? I don't know—"

"Oh, come on. You can do it."

"But with a *person?*" Maia stepped back again and bumped into the wall. "What if I can't bring you back?"

"Maia. Stop." Miranda grabbed her shoulders. "It's just like the pen. Come on, you made half the room disappear. You can handle lil ol' me."

Maia let out a heavy breath and took Miranda's hand.

It was easier than she'd thought it would be.

A few minutes later, Chloe appeared in the

doorway and knocked on the frame, gasping at what she saw—or, actually, *didn't* see—in the room.

"Hello?" she called out, unwilling to walk in over the invisible floor.

Maia pulled back her power, and the room reappeared, followed by Miranda and herself, her cousin gripping her hand tightly.

"That's—" Chloe was at a loss for words.

"Amazing!" Miranda finished, twirling around before she collapsed on the bed. "Amazing is what it is. I mean, it's so weird being on that side, you know? Because I could see me—and you—" she pointed to Maia. "—but you couldn't see us!" She pointed at Chloe. "What a cool power. I'm totally jealous."

Chloe entered the room, placing each foot gingerly on the floor like she half expected it to disappear before her eyes. "You seem to have gotten the hang of it quickly," she told Maia.

She shrugged. "Once I figured out what it felt like, it was pretty easy."

Chloe nodded. "Right."

"Something wrong?" Miranda asked, propping her head on her fist. "You seem weird."

"I called Aunt Cara last night," she replied. "Asked her about my mom."

"About her being the Seer?" Miranda sat up, her attention captured. "What did she say?"

Chloe relayed the message her mother had sent from beyond the grave.

"Wow," Maia said, dropping into Miranda's desk chair. "So it's all true."

"It seems so," Chloe replied.

"And that's all she said?" Miranda asked. "The Order is real. You're the Seer . . . blah blah blah. Not very useful, is it?" She winced at her own tone. "Sorry."

Chloe shrugged. "I can't say I hadn't hoped for something a little more helpful," she admitted. "But all I can assume is that she told me what she could. What she believed I needed to hear to go forward."

Miranda reached out and squeezed her hand. "She was right," she said. "You know now that it's true. That you're the Seer. So, we know we can trust your visions and what's in the journal."

"And now we can make a plan," Maia added. "Train and prepare, just like we said."

Chloe nodded. "Right," she said, her own confidence boosted by that of her friends. "Exactly. Now, we move forward and we do what needs to be done."

The three of them exchanged a look.

"Which is what, exactly?" Miranda asked.

Chloe sighed. "I have no idea."

It only took a few moments for them all to burst into laughter, breaking the tension.

"Guess we'll figure it out as we go along," Maia said.

By the time eight o'clock rolled around, Maia wasn't sure if there was anything she *couldn't* make disappear. After she'd blinked Miranda out of sight and back a half dozen times, she'd practiced with additional items: the desk and chair, the bed, the couch in the living room. Pretty soon, she could control other things as easily as her own body. And she didn't even have to touch them—at least not with a hand. As far as she could tell, anything that was in contact with her body— via the floor, the wall, the air—she could affect, although she wasn't certain just how far she could reach with her power.

It was something she was looking forward to trying at the practice field where she'd be less limited in what she could make disappear.

She was pretty sure if the whole house vanished, the neighbors might take notice.

But the field was relatively isolated, tucked behind the college campus and surrounded on three sides by trees. As long as nobody took a late night trip out to take a jog around the field, the group should have no problems training undisturbed.

It was fully dark by the time they arrived, but the security lights had kicked on, providing enough visibility for them to work without drawing attention.

When Maia and Miranda arrived, Chloe and Ethan were standing in the middle of the field, talking quietly. They didn't notice them at first, and Ethan reached up and stroked her cheek, kissing her softly. Maia felt uncomfortable trespassing on such an intimate moment, but Miranda had no such qualms.

She cleared her throat loudly. "Hey, get a room!"

Chloe rolled her eyes, but took Ethan's hand, lacing their fingers together as they turned toward them.

"Shut up," she said, but the words were without heat. "How'd it go after I left?"

"Amazing," Miranda replied. "She's come a long way. It's incredible!"

"Oh, yeah?" Chloe eyed Maia with interest. "I can't wait to see."

Voices in the distance drew their attention and in a moment Beck, Wren, and another familiar figure came around the corner of the bleachers.

"What's Professor Kennedy doing here?" Maia asked.

"I invited him," Miranda replied. "Turns out the good professor has a fifth degree black belt in Brazilian jiu-jitsu." At Ethan's wide-eyed look, her grin widened. "He's here to train those of us who don't have superhuman powers, so we can try not to get our butts kicked."

"Along with some of us who do have powers," Chloe said, nudging her with an elbow, "but who still need help with said not-butt-kicking."

"I think everyone could probably use some help with that," Beck said as they reached the group, forming a loose circle in the middle of the field. "Professor, I think you know everyone now, except Chloe and Ethan."

Professor Kennedy nodded, shaking Ethan's hand, then Chloe's. "The Seer," he said with a smile. "I've been looking forward to meeting you."

"Thanks for all your help so far," she replied politely before turning to the rest of the group.

"Well, for now, I think it makes sense for you all —" She waved toward Beck, Wren and Maia, "—to work on your gifts in a bigger arena . . . let you spread your wings, or whatever. Ethan, Miranda, and I will work with Professor Kennedy for a crash course in self-defense. If that's okay with you, Professor?"

"Of course," he said. "I'm here to help however I can."

It was strange for Maia to see Professor Kennedy in something other than tweed and ties. He wore a pair of baggy sweats, a loose t-shirt with the faded logo of an

'80s band, and well-worn sneakers. He arched a brow when he saw Maia staring.

"Sorry," she said. "I just—it's kind of weird learning your professor is a secret expert in martial arts."

He laughed. "Well, I'm no expert. I started taking jiu-jitsu with my son when he was in elementary school. It was to teach him discipline, help him focus, but it turned out I liked it as much as he did."

"So, do you think you can teach us how to protect ourselves?" Chloe asked.

"Well, I guess that's what we're here to find out," he said.

He led Chloe, Ethan, and Miranda to the far end of the field, while Wren, Beck, and Maia stayed in the center. Maia was curious about what Professor Kennedy was teaching them—she kind of wanted to learn some moves herself—but she was quickly drawn out of her thoughts when Wren disappeared before her eyes.

"I guess we're starting," Beck murmured.

Wren reappeared on Beck's other side. Maia figured two could play at that game.

She let the power flow through her, disappearing was as easy as breathing now, and smiled to herself when Wren and Beck stared at the spot where she'd been standing a few seconds before. She reappeared behind them and tapped them both on the shoulders.

"Wow, that's cool," Beck said with a grin as he spun around. "You've been practicing."

Maia grinned right back at him. "Just wait, you ain't seen nothing yet."

Chloe lay on her back, trying to catch her breath as she watched the stars appear and disappear as the clouds drifted past.

"Are you okay?" Ethan asked, shooting a glare at Professor Kennedy. "Did you have to throw her so hard?"

"I'm fine," Chloe said, sitting up. "Don't get mad at him. He's just trying to teach us."

"Teach us, fine," Ethan said. "But—"

"No buts," Chloe snapped. "We don't know how much time we have, so we need to learn quickly." She stood up and brushed the dirt off her jeans. "Believe me, I won't make *that* mistake again."

Ethan didn't look convinced, but he held his tongue.

"All right," the professor said. "Miranda, you try."

The two of them faced each other, arms up and legs braced in the *ready* stance Professor Kennedy had taught them.

"I'm going to come at you," he said. "Remember,

don't try to throw me. Just use my own body weight and momentum."

Miranda nodded and licked her lips, watching for his move. He moved toward her slowly and she dodged to the left, grabbed his arm and bent his thumb back.

"Good," he said. "What's next?"

He led her through a few more moves in slow motion, then speeding up until they flowed effortlessly from one to the other. Ethan went through the same drills, then the professor had the two of them practice against each other while he turned to Chloe.

"Ready to try again?" he asked.

She took up the ready position and nodded.

And then the world turned upside down and Professor Kennedy vanished. As did Miranda and Ethan. Chloe gasped, her heart pounding as she realized she was no longer on the practice field, but surrounded by a thick blanket of darkness. She couldn't see anything around her, only a stifling silence.

And she couldn't move. She struggled against invisible bonds, unable to scream, unable to do anything but search the darkness around her for some sign of life.

Some sign of *something*.

She was wrapped tightly and couldn't draw a deep breath—only shallow pants swallowed up by the blackness around her. Panic set in. What was happening? Where was she?

Just when she thought she couldn't take another minute, when she thought for sure she was going insane, the world reappeared and she drew a deep, gulping breath and fell to her knees.

"Chloe, are you okay?" Miranda appeared before her and she looked up, blinking at Ethan and Professor Kennedy who were watching her with concern.

"What happened?" Chloe asked, still gasping for air and confused. "I—I thought—"

Professor Kennedy bent over, his hands on his knees. "Did you see something?"

She nodded. "It seemed so real."

"You had a vision?" Ethan asked. "Without the window?"

"That's never happened before," she told the professor, and they all looked to the older man for answers.

"It appears your gift is growing," he said. "The window—the house—served as a kind of conduit for your visions. Most likely, they'll still be stronger and easier to access through the window, but it looks like it's not entirely necessary."

Chloe huffed. "Apparently not. Scared the crap out of me, I'm not going to lie." She didn't like the idea that she could be swept up in a vision like that.

"What did you see?" Ethan asked.

"Darkness," she replied. "I felt confined. Tied up.

Unable to breathe." Her heart rate sped up at the memory. "It was—pretty terrifying, actually."

Miranda wrapped an arm over her shoulders. "Maybe we should call it a night."

"No," Chloe said, getting to her feet. "We need to train, and I'm okay. Or I will be in a minute, anyway."

"Are you sure?" Ethan asked.

She nodded. "It just took me by surprise, is all."

Professor Kennedy pursed his lips, considering. "From what I understand, the Seer's visions can be quite intense. It's important to try and remember that it is a vision—that it isn't *really* happening. Your reactions are stimulated by the experience, but they can be controlled."

"You're saying what I felt was all in my head?"

"The mind is a powerful thing," the professor replied. "I don't claim to understand it all, but from what I've read, you can train yourself to be an observer —like when you see the vision in the window—instead of experiencing the vision."

"Well, that sounds good to me," Chloe said. "I'd be happy never to feel *that* ever again."

"I'll go through the journal with Miranda and high-light some specific passages that may help," Professor Kennedy said. "In the meantime, are you ready to get back to training?"

Chloe only thought about it for a moment. What

she'd seen in her vision had frightened her, and it was something she never wanted to experience again—not in a vision, and not in real life. She wasn't sure exactly how to prevent it, but she knew that learning to fight could only help.

"I'm ready," she said with a firm nod. "Bring it on."

THIRTEEN

"Okay, you guys ready?" Chloe shouted, standing shoulder to shoulder with Ethan, Miranda, and Professor Kennedy about twenty yards from Beck, Wren, and Maia.

Maia took a deep breath, reached to feel her power, and smiled when it responded instantly.

"Ready!" she shouted.

"Don't take it easy on us," Ethan said, setting his feet apart and crouching down a little, bracing himself.

"No risk of that," Beck said, cracking his neck as he rolled his shoulders. "You won't even see us coming." He winked at Maia and she heard Wren giggle on her other side.

"You guys ready?" Maia said, so only the other two could hear.

Wren and Beck nodded once. Then Maia took a deep breath and the three of them disappeared.

"Whoa!" Chloe said.

Miranda laughed. "I told you!"

Maia could see them both, of course—could see Wren running around behind the others while Beck headed straight for Ethan. To her surprise, Ethan seemed to sense him coming, and just when Beck leaned forward to grab him in a tackle, Ethan stepped nimbly to the side and used Beck's own momentum to throw him onto his back.

Ethan grinned and high-fived Professor Kennedy as Beck got slowly to his feet.

Maia relaxed her power and the three of them reappeared. "How'd you do that?" she asked. "Did you see him?"

Ethan shrugged. "Not really. But I could hear his footsteps as he ran. I could tell he was coming for me. Not that that's really a surprise." He held out a fist to Beck, who tapped it and smiled.

"Well, that sucks," Wren said, crossing her arms over her chest. "I didn't even get to try my gift."

"Let's go again," Beck said, brushing off his pants. "I think . . ." He paused at the sound of sirens—a lot of sirens—passing by beyond the trees. "I wonder what's going on."

"Maybe we should go check it out," Ethan said slowly.

"I don't think that's a good idea," Professor Kennedy replied. "You aren't ready yet."

Another siren passed by. In the distance they could make out shouts and screams. Breaking glass. Was that a gunshot?

"It sounds like all hell is breaking loose," Wren said.

"Well, according to what we've learned, it kind of is," Maia replied with a glance at the professor.

He nodded. "It's how the enemy is gaining power," he said. "He thrives on the violence . . . craves it."

"Well, then we need to stop him, don't we?" Chloe asked. "If we can keep him from feeding, maybe we can keep him from getting stronger."

"I'm telling you, you're not ready yet," the professor snapped. "If he—"

Screeching tires interrupted his tirade, followed by more shouts and breaking glass. Beck took off running toward the campus.

"I don't think we have a choice," he said over his shoulder. "It sounds like he's bringing the fight to us."

The group followed Beck as the sound of fighting grew louder. They plastered themselves along the brick wall of the library, and Beck darted a glance around the corner.

"What do you see?" Chloe whispered.

"Fighting," he replied. "Lots of fighting." He nodded at Ethan. "Let's go check it out."

When Wren started to follow them, Beck stopped. "You guys should wait here."

"Oh, no, I don't think so," she said, crossing her arms over her chest as they all started to talk at once.

"It could be danger—"

"—start with this macho bull—"

"—keep you *safe*—"

"—can take care of myself!"

"Guys!" Maia held up her hands. "This isn't doing any good. If anything, it's what he—*it*—wants."

"She's right," Professor Kennedy said. "It thrives on conflict."

They stood in a half-circle, hidden by the wall from the fighting beyond. The glares receded, deep breaths were taken, and after a moment, Beck muttered, "Sorry."

The sentiment was echoed around the group, and Maia nodded. "Good. Okay then. We go together." Beck's lips tightened, but he said nothing. She reached for her gift, smiling as the glow over her skin spread slowly out over the others. She heard the collective gasp and smiled wider, even though nobody could see it.

"Just because we're going into the lion's den doesn't mean we have to do it with guns blazing," she said. "I'll keep everyone hidden for as long as I can."

They rounded the corner, tense and watching, as they drew closer to the brawling crowd.

Maia had thought that even though they were invisible, that those influenced—or possessed—would be able to sense them somehow, but nobody seemed to even notice them.

The central quad was a violent free-for-all, as a crowd of about fifty people, battered and bloody, pounded on each other in no logical pattern. A short man to the left kicked another man lying on the ground, then turned just in time to lurch forward and drive his head into yet another man's stomach. Maia watched in awed horror at the melee surrounding her.

Their eyes were the creepiest thing of all, filmed over with a shifting darkness—the sign of influence that Wren had told her about.

"What do we do?" Miranda asked quietly. "We can't hurt them. They don't even know what they're doing."

A body suddenly slammed into Maia, knocking her to the ground and she grunted at the impact. She lay there for a moment, stunned, and her gift retreated, leaving everyone around her visible.

"Wren!" she shouted, pulling herself to her feet. She'd have to freeze time so Maia could get herself centered. "Watch out!"

Wren nodded at her and Maia saw her take a deep

breath, readying herself to access her gift, but Beck grabbed her wrist, stopping her.

"Wait," he said.

The group gathered closer in the center of the chaos, back to back and tensed for a fight. Maia watched the madness around her—a group of three pounding on a young man lying on the ground; two women rolling around, fists tightly clenched in each other's hair; a teenage boy with a lighter gleefully starting a dumpster fire.

"Why aren't they attacking?" Chloe asked.

"I don't know," Beck replied. "It's like they don't even see us." He shot a sideways look at Maia, but she shrugged.

"It's not me," she said.

They all looked toward Professor Kennedy. He frowned. "I think . . . It's accumulating power." At their blank expressions, he continued. "Using the anger and violence to boost its strength. I would say It doesn't want to face off against all of you until It's ready."

The boy with the lighter threw it down and jumped on a skinny man with scrapes on both arms. Maia jumped back as they fell to the ground at her feet.

"Well, he might not want to fight us, but we need to stop this," Chloe said. "We can't let these people kill each other!"

As if on cue, the madness stopped. The crashes

and screams abruptly cut off, leaving only heavy breathing and the quiet crackling of lighter-boy's fire.

"This is weird," Miranda said quietly. "It's weird, right?"

"Definitely weird," Maia replied.

The people, who had only moments before been trying to annihilate each other, stood and turned to face them, forming a loose circle facing inward, as the new Order faced outward.

"What in the world is going on?" Beck asked the professor.

The older man let out a heavy breath. "I have no idea."

The two groups stood, staring at each other, tense and unmoving. Then the crowd parted in front of Maia, and a woman walked through the gap.

She was older, maybe forty? Fifty? Maia could see evidence that she'd once been attractive, but her brown skin was faded and dry, like old leather, and her unkempt hair and disheveled clothing was in direct contrast to her erect bearing. She walked with confidence, like a woman in charge.

The group of fighters looked to her, even stepping back a little deferentially. She smiled, and Maia heard a collective gasp among her friends.

"What?" she asked.

Miranda leaned in to answer, but the woman's dark eyes—*How were they so dark?*— zeroed in on Maia.

"Ah, the new girl," she said. "I don't believe I've had the pleasure."

"Gina," Beck said, warning in his tone.

"Shh, baby. Mommy's talking," she replied with a wink.

Maia gasped, looking to Miranda for confirmation. She nodded grimly.

"You are *not* my mother," he spat back. "You're not even Gina."

"Oh, au contraire," she said, walking leisurely around the group to stand in front of Beck. "Your dear mother is in here. She just has a little company."

"Why don't you get out and pick on someone your own size," Beck growled.

"Well, we tried that, didn't we?" she said, running a finger down his cheek. "Didn't go so well. Besides, she likes me in here." Her smile dropped and she curled a fist in his shirt. "Unlike *some* people who don't know how to appreciate a gift."

Beck snorted. "Gift? Yeah, right. No thanks."

Her fist tightened, twisting in the fabric as she all but spat in his face. "You always were a disobedient child."

Wren stepped forward and shoved Gina back.

"Why don't you quit with all the games and tell us what you want?"

Gina grinned. "What I want? Oh, I think you already know the answer to that question."

"Power," Chloe replied. "But why? What do you want to do with it?"

"Oh now, that's for me to know and you to find out," she said in a sing-songy voice. She leaned in and whispered something in Chloe's ear. Maia couldn't hear what she said, but Chloe let out a stifled cry and lunged at Gina, who jumped back with a laugh. The hair pulling women and lighter-boy stepped between them, blocking Chloe. She pushed against them, but Ethan took her wrist, stilling her.

"Not now," he said.

"Nope, not now," Gina parroted, continuing to step backward. Black smoke poured from her finger-tips, billowing around them. "But soon, my lovelies. Very soon." She turned to walk away, disappearing around the corner of the building. In groups of two or three, the rioters moved away as well, vanishing in the cloud of smoke and the surrounding darkness. Within minutes, only Maia and her friends were left in the quad as the smoke dissipated, floating away in the slight breeze.

"Well, that could have gone better," Beck muttered.

"Nobody died," Wren replied. "I count that as a win."

"But none of this makes any sense." Miranda threw up her hands. "I get that it wants to feed or whatever, but why bring all those people out here? Just to gloat at us?"

"The thing does seem like a bit of a show-off," Maia said. "Likes to have an audience, maybe?"

"I think it's more than that," Professor Kennedy said slowly, eyes narrowed like he was working out a puzzle. "It's trying to get in your heads. Not directly. It's not strong enough—Beck proved that. But It wants you to know It's watching. It knows where you are. Knows what you're doing. And It's not worried . . . at all."

Miranda bumped Chloe's arm. "What did Gina say to you, anyway?"

"What?"

"When she whispered in your ear?"

Chloe shrugged, looking at the ground. "You know, typical stuff. *You'll never defeat me* kind of garbage." Maia thought maybe she was missing something when Miranda gave her a long look, but she let it drop.

"So It's trying to psych us out," Beck said.

"Well, It's doing a good job!" Miranda snapped. "How are we supposed to prepare for this epic fight if

It's watching our every move and is always one step ahead of us?"

"We have to be more careful," Chloe replied, voice calm despite her trembling hands. She clenched them into fists at her sides. "We don't let It see. We have Wren and now Maia. They can keep us hidden when we need to be."

Ethan unfurled her fingers and took her hand in his. "We now know that It's watching, so we'll make sure there's nothing to see."

"Will that work?" Wren asked Professor Kennedy. "Can It, I don't know, sense us somehow?"

He frowned. "From what I've read in the journal, It can, to a certain extent—but only if It's focused on looking."

"So, we don't give It reason to look," Beck said with a shrug. "It seems like It's using its lackeys to keep an eye on us, so when we need to be one place, we'll just let them think we're in another."

"Easy enough," Wren said. She nodded at Maia. "We can take care of that."

"We'll need to find another place to train, though," Chloe said. "Obviously, the practice field is too exposed. We need something more remote."

"I'd offer my place," the professor said, "but they've seen me with you, so I'm sure I'll be watched as well, if I'm not already."

"How about the quarry?" Ethan suggested.

Chloe shook her head. "Too much traffic."

"The park's too exposed." Beck started to pace. "The old airport might work."

"They're starting construction on a bunch of new homes near there," Miranda said. "I saw it in the paper. People will be all over the place."

Maia cleared her throat. "I think I might know a place."

They all looked at her in surprise. She was new in town, so it was understandable.

"It's isolated, but not far from our place—maybe an hour's hike?" she said. "I found it when I first got to town and I've been out there a couple times since, when I needed to get away and think about, you know, things." She shrugged. "I've never seen anyone else out there. I think it could work, maybe."

The group exchanged questioning glances, then seemed to shrug in unison.

"Worth a shot," Chloe said. "First thing in the morning, let's go check it out."

"How did you find this place, anyway?" Chloe asked, clinging to Maia's left hand while Ethan held her other one and Miranda took up the rear in their odd human chain. Maia had assured her that they didn't need to be touching for her power to render them all invisible, but Chloe thought it was better to be safe than sorry. It was probably putting her gift to the test anyway. They'd been walking for almost forty-five minutes and Miranda said the longest Maia had gone was thirty.

She didn't seem tired, though. If anything, she seemed energized; as if happy she had found a purpose in the group. She navigated the overgrown trail easily, dodging overhanging branches and hopping over fallen logs, and Chloe found herself breathing heavily as she tried to keep up.

Maia glanced back at Chloe and opened her mouth to respond to her question, but Miranda hissed from the back of the line.

"Don't distract her!"

Maia rolled her eyes. "I'm fine. Really. It's like a faucet—once I figured out how to turn it on and off, regulating the flow is pretty easy." She looked back at Chloe again before turning to step over a root. "I've always been a hiker, but didn't really get to do it much in Seattle. When I moved here, I got out as much as I could to try and explore. I had no idea this trail even existed . . . just stumbled across it one day."

Chloe wasn't sure she believed in chance anymore, but didn't say anything.

"So you two are cousins," Ethan said. "Were you close as kids?"

Maia laughed. "Miranda hated me."

"I did not!" Miranda retorted. "I just thought you were so mean, at first. You wouldn't even talk to me."

"How old were you?" Ethan asked.

"Twelve. Miranda was ten."

"You're only two years older than us, and you're already in grad school?" Chloe stumbled over a root and Ethan caught her. "I didn't realize that."

"She's a brainiac," Miranda said. "Two years of college while she was in high school and still graduated at the top of her class."

Maia kept her gaze forward, but Chloe could make out the hint of embarrassed color in her cheeks.

"Anyway," she said. "I came out to stay with Miranda and her mom when my parents got divorced. It was a tough time, obviously, and my mom—well, my mom was dealing with her own stuff and so I was kind of in my own head a lot, you know."

"Must have been rough," Chloe said quietly. Maia shrugged, but said nothing else.

"Are we there yet?" Miranda whined loudly, breaking the tension.

Maia laughed. "Almost. Just around this next bend."

Wren, Beck, and Professor Kennedy would be

waiting for them, most likely. Or would get there soon after? Chloe wasn't sure. It was weird to think that Chloe and the others would be frozen in time as Wren's group passed them by. Maia had given Wren directions and drawn a rough map and Wren was confident she could get Beck and the professor there, hidden by her own power.

As far as anyone watching was concerned, Beck and Wren were at her house, Chloe and Ethan were at the Alpha house, and Miranda and Maia were at home. Sure, it was a little unusual for them all to still be in town when Christmas break was already underway, but not unheard of. The actual holiday was still a week away, and there were more than a few students milling around town, working last minute shifts to make a little extra holiday money or just hanging out with their friends.

It took some planning and coordination to figure out who would go where to get who, but they worked it out. Two groups—one invisible, thanks to Maia, the other moving through a world suspended in time, thanks to Wren—and they'd join up once they'd reached the place that Maia told them about. A safe place to train, away from Chaos' minions.

Chloe hoped so, at least. They decided to wait until they got where they were going to let down their guard a bit.

Sure enough, they rounded the corner and Wren and the others were standing just a few feet ahead at what looked like the top of a hill. Maia released Chloe's hand and Wren startled in surprise, then smiled and waved as they all came into sight once again.

"Took you long enough," Beck said crossing his beefy arms over his chest with a smirk.

"Shut up," Chloe said, without heat. "*Some* of us are bound by the laws of physics. Well, time at least. Besides—"

The words fell from her lips as they arrived at the hilltop and she saw what lay beyond.

Or rather, saw it *again*.

At her feet, the ground dropped down to a large clearing surrounded by trees. Dried grass swayed in the breeze, the sparkling early morning sunshine cutting through sparse clouds overhead creating an almost idyllic portrait.

It was a startling contrast to how Chloe had always seen the clearing—filled with the sights and sounds of battle and bloodshed, thick black smoke hovering over the ground and twisting into a wild tornado of destruction on the far side.

Despite the differences, she was sure it was the same clearing. And despite her efforts to ignore them, Gina's hissed words echoed in her brain—words whispered in a gleeful threat that she dared not repeat to anyone. That was something she'd need to figure out how to deal with on her own. And from the looks of things, she'd better figure it out quickly.

"Chloe?" Ethan squeezed her hand. "What's wrong?"

For a moment, she wondered if she was once again caught in a vision, if reality had been pushed aside for a peek at the future. "Do you see it?" she whispered.

"See what?" Ethan asked.

"The clearing?" She pointed. "The woods?"

Ethan looked at her in concern. "Of course I see it. Chlo, what's wrong?"

She swallowed the lump in her throat and the reflexive terror in her bones.

"This is it," she said.

"What?"

She tore her gaze from the clearing; the images from the vision melting into the current landscape and out again. She looked into the concerned faces of her friends, filled with the sudden urge to take them all and run back home. Pretend they'd never found it. Pretend it never happened—*would* never happen.

But she knew better. More than anyone else, Chloe knew there was no escaping their joint future.

So, although she couldn't paint on a smile, she forced what she hoped was a look of grim determination onto her face. One that hid the fear making her insides tremble and her heart pound heavily in her chest.

"This is where it happens," she said. "This is where we fight."

Chloe was on the verge of sleep when she heard movement downstairs and muffled voices. She was already sitting up when Maia knocked lightly on her door and poked her head in.

"Someone's here to see you."

She glanced at her alarm clock. "It's two in the morning."

Maia arched an eyebrow. "I have a feeling you won't want to miss this."

It had been a long day training, followed by another long hike home. They'd made some progress, though. The self-defense with Professor Kennedy was coming along—Chloe was even able to throw Ethan onto his back, so she felt pretty good about that, even though she hurt her shoulder in the process. The professor said she'd get better at it with practice.

Beck was finally able to put his strength through its paces—throwing boulders and hefting fallen logs around the clearing just to see what he could do.

He was fast, too. They had yet to time him, but

Chloe could barely follow his progress when he ran at full speed. That had to come in handy at some point.

Maia, though. Maia was amazing. Her power seemed almost limitless—and incredibly precise. She could vanish a tree from forty feet away—and the entire group, even when they scattered themselves around the clearing. It took focus, though. So they'd need to figure out how to best use her gift, as well.

They were still working on a plan, but for the first time she felt confident that they'd come up with one.

Stifling a yawn and stretching out her aching shoulder, Chloe slipped out of bed and found Miranda rubbing her eyes as she emerged from her own room.

"What's going on?" she asked.

Chloe shrugged and they both followed Maia downstairs. Chloe was surprised to find Dylan—the barista from the coffee shop—dressed in a ratty t-shirt, plaid pajama pants, and socks that looked soaking wet, standing awkwardly by the front door.

"Dylan? Is everything okay? Did something happen to your dad?" Miranda asked.

"His dad?" Chloe asked.

Miranda looked at her, blinking. "I didn't realize—" She shook her head. "Dylan's Professor Kennedy's son."

Chloe couldn't even find it in herself to be surprised at the connection. "Is he okay?" she asked.

"My dad?" Dylan replied, confusion creasing his brow. "Yeah, he's fine. Why would something be wrong with him?" He ran a hand through his hair which was already standing on end. "I . . . I don't know. I'm not even sure what I'm doing here."

"Did you . . . did you *walk* all the way here?"

Dylan shrugged. "I guess? I mean . . . I woke up and I was on your front step."

Chloe exchanged a look with Maia, who sighed. "I know the feeling." She turned to head to the kitchen. "Anyone want tea? Something stronger? I know I sure do."

Dylan watched her go, his mouth hanging open. "Is she okay? I mean, other than having a strange guy show up on your doorstep in the middle of the night."

Chloe let out a short laugh. "Yeah, well. Believe it or not, this isn't the weirdest thing that's happened around here lately."

"That's putting it mildly," Miranda said, shuffling past them without looking at either of them and curled up in the chair, wrapping the afghan around her shoulders. "Let me guess," she said to Dylan. "You had a strange dream."

"Umm . . . yeah."

"And Chloe and/or this house figured prominently in said dream."

He glanced nervously at Chloe, then nodded. "Yeah."

"And then you ended up here and you're not exactly sure why, but you felt compelled, or drawn here or whatever."

"Yeah. What's this all about?"

Maia poked her head through the doorway. "Tea's ready. I found some cookies, too."

"No, wait," Dylan protested. "I want to know what's going on."

Chloe patted him on the shoulder. "You'll get your answers, but take the tea," she said. "Believe me, you're going to need it."

The Order faces the ultimate battle in...

Super Natural: The New Super Humans, Book Three.

Get your copy today!

SPECIAL
THANKS TO...

My editor, Kathie Spitz
My proofreader, Amy Gamache at Rose David Editing
My formatter, JC Clarke at The Graphics Shed
All the amazing authors of Enchanted Publications
The T.M. Franklin Book Club and T.M. Franklin
ARC Team

...and of course, to my wonderful family for their never
ending support.

ABOUT THE AUTHOR

T.M. Franklin writes stories of adventure, romance, & a little magic. A former TV news producer, she decided making stuff up was more fun than reporting the facts. Her first published novel, MORE, was born during National Novel Writing month, a challenge to write a novel in thirty days.

MORE was well-received, being selected as a finalist in the 2013 Kindle Book Review Best Indie Book Awards, as well as winning the Suspense/Thriller division of the Blogger Book Fair Reader's Choice Awards. She's since written novels in a variety of genres, as well as several best-selling short stories...and there's always more on the way.

Find out more at www.TMFranklin.com

And to be the first notified about upcoming

releases, sales, and giveaways, subscribe to
T.M. Franklin's newsletter at
www.TMFranklin.com/Subscribe. All new
subscribers get a FREE copy of
Unscheduled Departure!

ALSO
BY
T.M. FRANKLIN

The MORE Trilogy

"Reminiscent of the Mortal Instruments series... only better!"
– Penny Dreadful Reviews

MORE

The Guardians

TWELVE

The New Super Humans

Super Humans

Super Powers

Super Natural

Super Heroes

Standalone Books

A Fun and Quirky YA Romance

How to Get Ainsley Bishop to Fall in Love with You

Adventure and Romance on the High Seas

Cutlass

A Magical Holiday Romance

Second Chances

Visions of Sugar Plums

Short Stories

Unscheduled Departure

A Piece of Cake

Made in the USA
San Bernardino, CA
09 April 2019